# Smoke Screen

## Praise for *Smoke Screen*

★

Witty and deftly paced.... The author cleverly
balances the lighthearted with the thoughtful.
— ★PUBLISHERS WEEKLY STARRED REVIEW

Koss does an excellent job of expressing
how adolescents' minds work....
[A] comical page-turner.
— SCHOOL LIBRARY JOURNAL

## More AG Fiction
## for Intermediate Readers

★

*Stolen Words* by Amy Goldman Koss

*Sister Split* by Sally Warner

*Letters to Cupid* by Francess Lantz

*The Secret Voice of Gina Zhang* by Dori Jones Yang

*Nowhere, Now Here* by Ann Howard Creel

*A Ceiling of Stars* by Ann Howard Creel

*A Song for Jeffrey* by Constance M. Foland

*Going for Great* by Carolee Brockmann

AG
FICTION
TM

# Smoke Screen

## Amy Goldman Koss

American Girl®

### SCHOLASTIC INC.
New York  Toronto  London  Auckland  Sydney
Mexico City  New Delhi  Hong Kong  Buenos Aires

ISBN 0-439-38945-3

12 11 10 9 8 7 6 5 4 3 2                    2 3 4 5 6 7/0

Printed in the U.S.A.                                    23

First Scholastic printing, January 2002

Editorial Development: Andrea Weiss
Art Direction and Design: Joshua Mjaanes, Ingrid Slamer
Cover Illustration: Nancy Wolff

*To Roberta F. Levine, my Birdy.*
*Thanks also to Andrea Weiss, Linda Baker,*
*Ellen Slezak, Doreen Kirkwood,*
*Peter Williamson, Sandy Medof, and*
*Clara Rodriguez*

# Contents

# 1

# A Quit
# and a Smile

Dad handed each of us a glass of bubbly cider and began the countdown. "Five! . . . Four! . . . Three! . . . Two! . . ."

At "One!" my mother crumpled up her pack of cigarettes and struck a "Ta-Da!" pose.

Then, at the stroke of midnight, she crowed, "Happy New Year, folks! You are now looking at a nonsmoker!"

Huh? Everyone exchanged puzzled looks. Nonsmoker? Mom? No way. I could tell that my older brother, Les, was thinking the same thing. He was giving Mom his yeah-right-like-we-really-believe-that expression.

"No, really—I quit!" Mom insisted. "Starting now, forever!"

No one budged until finally Dad said, "That's fantastic, honey!" and gave Mom a big squeeze.

What the heck—maybe it was true. I whooped out a "YA-HOO!" and rushed over to hug and kiss Mom. My best friend, Birdy, did too. Les was way too cool for hugs and kisses, so he just grunted his approval. Then we all toasted Mom's fabulous news with our cider.

Back in my room after the toast, Birdy climbed straight up to my top bunk and pulled the blanket to her chin, meaning she was ready to go to sleep. "I never thought she'd quit," Birdy yawned.

"Me neither," I said. "Never!"

Birdy had always been my best friend, so she knew my mom almost as well as I did. But Birdy couldn't *really* know what it was like to have the only smoking mom left in the state of California.

"Hey, Birdy!" I said. "No more being dragged to the store at all hours pretending we're going for milk or toilet paper when my mother really just needs cigarettes! And no more . . . Birdy?"

She made a gurgley noise that meant she was ninety-eight and a half percent asleep and hadn't heard a word I said.

★ ★ ★

Mom was always up before the sun, humming and rattling around in the kitchen, smoking. But on New Year's Day she didn't come out of her room until practically noon.

Birdy and I were at the table eating what we'd just decided would become our traditional New Year's Day breakfast, Doritos dipped in chocolate pudding, when Mom came in and poured herself a cup of coffee. Instead of sitting down, though, she froze at the counter and just stood there, peering into her coffee mug.

Finally Mom came out of her trance and sighed. "A cup of coffee without a cigarette," she said, "is like a day without sunshine."

She blinked sadly at us. We blinked back.

Then Mom dumped her coffee into the sink. "A day without sunshine is like . . . well, it's like NIGHT!" She sighed and crept back to her room.

Birdy and I looked at each other and cracked up.

I didn't see Mom again until hours later, after Birdy had left. That's when I went to her room to ask where my pink sandals were. I found her lying in bed, glaring at the ceiling.

"How should I know?" she growled. "They're YOUR shoes for YOUR feet and YOU'RE responsible for them! Do I ever ask you to find MY pink sandals?"

"You don't have pink sandals," I said.

"That's not the point!" she barked.

"Well, you ask me to find your car keys," I said.

Mom glared darts at me. I tried to back out of her room, but she ordered me to stay and read American Cancer Society antismoking pamphlets to her. She wanted to hear about all the symptoms of nicotine withdrawal.

Mom's blinds were shut and it was hard to read in the dark, but when I reached for the light switch, she nearly bit off my head. How was I supposed to know that light hurt her eyes?

"READ!" she demanded.

"It says drowsiness and trouble sleeping," I told my tormentor.

"I have that—both of those," Mom mumbled.

"Trouble concentrating, irritability," I continued.

"Humph," she grouched, insulted by the idea that she might be grumpy.

When I finally escaped Mom's lair and came squinting into the light, Dad said, "Well, Mitzi, the first day is the worst."

But when Mom still hadn't come out of her room by the time I left for school the next morning, Dad had changed the refrain to, "The first FEW days are the worst."

Before he opened their bedroom door, I saw him

take a gulp of air, as if he were diving into cold, shark-infested waters.

After school I found Mom lying on the couch. I assumed that meant she was making progress. But then, instead of saying hello, she snarled, "I don't suppose anyone has fed the fish!"

If she hadn't been in such a foul mood, I would have told her about Mike Humphrey. I'd have told her about his hazel eyes (like mine) and tight brown curls (not like mine), and how, when he smiled, the corners of his mouth went ear to ear. That wide smile might not *sound* handsome, but it was. Mike Humphrey was also the fastest runner in the sixth grade and faster than a lot of kids in seventh.

He didn't know I was alive. Actually, until that day, I'd barely noticed *he* was alive. Our homeroom teacher, Ms. London, changed our seats every month, and she'd just put him next to me. One close-up look at him and I was a sweaty-palmed, weak-kneed goner!

But I couldn't tell any of that to this crabby non-smoker who'd snuck in and replaced my friendly old mother. So I fed the fish and went to my room to write *Jan. 2, M.H. next door!* in my diary. I wrote in code because my brother, Les, had been known to read my diary in search of things to get me in trouble for or tease me about.

There was only one person left whom I could tell about Mike, and that was Birdy. She and I weren't in the same class this year, so I wasn't sure if she even knew who he was. Now that we were in middle school, there were tons of kids we didn't know before.

I hid my diary and ran out the door. A big old church stands between my house and Birdy's. Over the years we had beaten a path across the church's lawn. I figured that was the punishment it deserved for being in our way.

Birdy's side door was never locked. I raced through her kitchen and up to her room, where I found her sanding a picture frame. Birdy was always doing stuff like that. Her mom ran an art supply store and dragged home all kinds of craftsy junk for Birdy.

The sound of sandpaper made my teeth itch, but I didn't complain, because I had Mike Humphrey on my mind.

Birdy put down the frame and examined her nails for a good one to chew on. "He's that runner, right?" she asked.

"OF COURSE he's that runner. He's MIKE HUMPHREY!"

"So, you like him?" she asked, attacking a corner of her thumb.

"When he smiles, his mouth opens from here to here." I sighed.

"He sounds like a muppet." Birdy laughed. "Kermit." She held up the frame and blew sawdust at me, making me sneeze. Then she went back to sanding (*scritch, scritch, scritch*) and said, "So, how's your mother doing with her quit?" which meant Birdy was done talking about Mike.

## 2

# Real Syrup and an Eyelash

The next morning, I tiptoed past the snoring, non-smoking grouch on the couch. Then I gagged down my father's idea of quote-unquote "breakfast" and escaped.

Once I was safely out of the house, I was able to concentrate on more important things, like wracking my brain for ways to get Mike Humphrey to notice me.

In class, I tried yawning loudly and rustling around in my seat, but that didn't work. Maybe he had a blind spot just my size and shape.

On Wednesday I went to the Girls' After-School Program at the YWCA. I used to go there only on the days Mom worked. She had a part-time job as a substitute teacher. Right now Mom was way too quitted-out to handle a room full of tiny brats, but I went to Girls' After-School anyway—just to get away from her.

I was semi-friends with an After-School girl named Fern, who rode my bus. Fern was also in Girl Scouts. She'd earned every possible badge from Brownies on up and wore her entire uniform, including the socks, on Scout days.

Anyway, Fern said boys like girls they can relax with. Her dad told her that men got married because they got tired of holding their stomachs in and having to burp quietly.

It didn't sound very romantic, but I decided to give it a try. I stole an orange off the tree near the bus stop and brought it to homeroom, where I casually tossed and caught it like one of the guys. Actually, I mostly tossed and chased it, until Ms. London made me put it away. Mike hadn't noticed anyway.

I'd never take Fern's boy-girl advice again.

I started keeping a log in my diary of what Mike wore every day to see if there was a pattern. I figured he'd notice me for sure if our clothes matched. But if I wore a blue shirt when he wore red, it didn't mean the day was shot. There were other possible cosmic connections, like if we coughed or sneezed at the same time.

My dad seemed to think that if he acted extra happy, we wouldn't notice what a grump Mom was being. Maybe he thought he was balancing out her gloominess. Whatever his thinking was, his cheerfulness was really ANNOYING—especially first thing in the morning. In this case, a Saturday morning.

"Isn't it wonderful that Mommy"—he was the only one in the family who still called her that— "has finally quit smoking?" chirped Mr. Cheerful, pouring orange juice and grinning.

"Yeah, wonderful," I grumbled.

I admit I'd nagged Mom for years about her smoking. I'd broken her cigarettes, thrown out her lighters, and hidden her ashtrays. But after five days of her sulks and temper tantrums, I secretly wished she'd just light up and act normal.

"Mitzi," Dad said, interrupting my thoughts, "this is an important thing Mommy is doing. We all have to do our best to help her. One day you'll laugh about these eggs."

Dad nodded in the direction of my plate, which was shoved in among his music books and papers on the kitchen table. The eggs looked just about as edible as his grubby stack of note cards.

"Eat your breakfast," he said, clearly struggling to keep his Mr. Cheerful act going.

Some disgusting drool was seeping out of the eggs and creeping across the plate to my burned toast. "Look at that," I said. "Would YOU eat it?"

"I just did," Dad said. He was working on his program notes. He's a violinist in the local symphony, and he writes the thing the ushers hand out about the conductors and composers and soloists. He lists all the musicians' names, including his own. He was on a deadline and wanted me to leave him alone. So, while he was busy writing his notes, I fed the slithery goo to the Sink Monster.

Then I snuck out to Birdy's. Her family has a yellow restaurant booth in their kitchen, and I was just in time to slide in next to Birdy for some French toast. Now *that* was a real breakfast. Birdy's mom, Miriam, was a great cook.

So there I sat, eating French toast with all the syrup and butter I wanted. Not some sorry sugar-free, flavor-free brown glop, but *real* syrup. And real butter, too, not the yellowish nonfat glue that I was force-fed at home.

"How's your mom's quit going?" Miriam asked.

"OK," I fibbed. "Day five."

"Sandy quit smoking," Miriam said to Birdy's

father, Milt, tapping the newspaper in front of his face. Milt smiled over the top of his paper. "Well, good luck to her!" he said and laughed in his big Santa Claus way.

Milt was always reading, unless he was watching TV with the volume cranked to the max. It drove Birdy nuts that he turned the television up so loud, but I thought it was funny.

I liked Birdy's mom, too. Miriam wore baggy dresses with wild prints and noisy earrings. Her short hair was snow-white. My brother said it turned white with fright when she first saw baby Birdy. He's such a dweeb.

After breakfast Birdy and I went up to her room. She pulled out her latest craft. This time it was rug-hooking. Milt's TV came on in the den, so I had to yell to Birdy that sitting next to Mike Humphrey was making me flunk. "I can't concentrate in class, and each day that he doesn't notice me, I get more irritable. Plus I'm tired because I'm awake all night trying to figure out how to get him to like me before our seats are switched for February." I sighed. "Love's giving me all of the symptoms in the quit-smoking pamphlets!"

"Maybe it's because you're quitting smoking too, sort of," Birdy replied. "You know, second-hand smoke and all that?"

"Well, at least I'm not going as nuts as my mom. She's totally wacko. This morning she came out of her room to announce that she hates our doorknobs. How can anyone possibly care enough about doorknobs to hate them?"

"Hmmm." Birdy's attention was on her rug-hooking.

"And I don't know why she's so worried about doorknobs when the rest of the house is such a total mess," I said.

"Maybe YOU should clean it up," Birdy said.

"Me?"

Birdy put down her rug-hooking stuff and said, "I bet it would cheer up your mom. Come on, I'll help." And she dragged me back across the churchyard to my house.

Birdy looked around the kitchen, sizing up the job. She did a lot more housework at her house than I did at mine, so she knew about that kind of stuff.

"I'm the head of the Sultan's harem," Birdy whispered. "I have to train you before the Sultan gets back." Birdy and I like to pretend a lot, especially when we have to do unbearably dull chores like cleaning. "If there's a single speck of dirt anywhere," she continued, "the Sultan will have us both killed."

"And they'll dump us in the desert with no water," I added.

"On a flea-bitten old camel."

Birdy pointed to my dad, buried in his pile of books. "He's the Sultan's official snitch. So haul those newspapers out to the recycle bin before he sees you slacking off."

Birdy got the vacuum cleaner and started in on the den. After about two seconds, Mom charged out of her room. She was wearing ratty old sweats, and her hair was going every which way. "STOP THAT RACKET!" she shrieked. Birdy's fingers flew to her mouth. Then she shut off the vacuum. "All I ask for is a little PEACE AND QUIET!" Mom snarled. "Is that too much to ASK?"

Birdy started winding up the vacuum cord. Her freckles were so bright they looked like sparks.

Mom stomped back to her room and slammed the door. *Bam!*

I looked at Birdy. Birdy looked at me. We both started to giggle. "I thought you were exaggerating!" Birdy sputtered.

January was zooming by. My mom was acting loony, and I had made zero impression on Mike Humphrey. It was totally irritating being in love with someone who didn't notice me.

But on January tenth at 9:48 A.M., I got an eyelash or something in my eye and started to cry. Not a wailing, snot-pouring boo-hoo—just tears. By some miracle, Mike noticed and said, "You OK?"

"I'm fine," I gasped. In my head I was screaming, "HE'S TALKING TO ME AND OUR OUTFITS DON'T EVEN MATCH!" My palms got clammy and my stomach jumped. But then he started to look away, so I quickly added, "I'm fine but . . . um, my mom's not."

"Huh?" he asked.

"My mom," I stammered, trying to keep his attention. "She's . . . sick." I pictured Mom lying in bed, overcome by every withdrawal symptom in the book. A quit-bed looked remarkably like a sickbed in my mind's eye.

Mike looked blank.

"We don't know *how* sick yet," I quickly added. "She's . . . um, taking medical tests."

He nodded as if he really cared. It was incredible! I smiled bravely—the worried but hopeful, loving daughter. Surely Mike Humphrey would admire such a girl.

Maybe saying Mom was sick wasn't the world's greatest idea, but I vowed to myself that I'd make up for it by being extra sweet to her when I got home. What *should* I have said? I was crying over war? World hunger? An eyelash? Any of those would have sounded dumb.

When it was time to leave for my next class, I walked in a tall, brave, stoic way—like a hero in a war movie. I hoped Mike noticed.

# 3
## The Balcony and a Close Call

I couldn't wait to tell Birdy about my conversation with Mike Humphrey, but a popular girl named Roxy Gold-something was sitting next to her on the bus that afternoon. Birdy looked absolutely dazzled to be sitting next to Roxy. I didn't growl at them or show in any way how cruddy it felt to have Roxy's butt where my butt belonged. I just sat somewhere else.

When we got off the bus, I could tell Birdy was dying to talk about sitting with Roxy. I knew she wanted me to act impressed so she could pretend it was no big deal. Instead, I told her Mike Humphrey had spoken to me.

But when she asked me what Mike had said, I clammed up.

"Well, did he say, 'You're standing on my foot'?"

"Nothing like that," I muttered. "I can't remember EXACTLY what he said." I hoped that sounded mysterious. Let Birdy think Mike and I had talked about so many things that I just couldn't remember them all. I bet she remembered every word Roxy had said!

By this time we were standing in front of my house. I wondered what new horror Mom's quit had in store for me. "Wanna come over?" I asked, sort of begging. Birdy hadn't stepped through our door since the vacuum cleaner incident.

"No thanks," she said. "I have tons of home-work, and I have some ribbons that I want to sew together to make a little purse. Doesn't that sound incredibly cute?"

I wondered if she had finished the rug or the picture frame yet, but I didn't ask. Being best friends with someone your whole life, you learn what not to ask.

The first thing I heard when I went inside was my mom humming. That was a sound I hadn't heard in precisely ten days. I crept closer and smelled smoke. Where there's smoke, there's—a cigarette. I turned down the hall and saw Mom, dressed in real clothes with her hair combed. She was standing there sorting the mail and smoking.

"Here's another one for you," she said cheerfully to the fish tank. She'd named our two fish Resident and Occupant and liked to joke that they got more mail than she did. I watched her take a deep drag.

"HEY!" I yelled. "What are you doing?"

She made a sheepish "Oh, well" face at me, puffing out an enormous smoke ring.

"You mean we put up with your crabby nastiness for NOTHING?" That was me, getting really mad now. Mom shuffled her feet but didn't put out her cigarette. I stomped away and added some door slamming for extra effect.

That night there was silence at home, the kind that screamed, "NO ONE IS SPEAKING TO ANYONE HERE!" Birdy said my parents didn't invent it. She said it's called "the silent treatment" and it's famous. But by the next morning life was back to normal again, meaning hummy, rattly, and smoky.

In the Y bathroom that afternoon, during Girls' After-School, I was perfecting my brave-sensitive smile when Fern came in.

"Got a stomachache?" she asked.

"No," I said, changing my expression. "*This* is my stomachache face." I made my eyes go droopy and my mouth sag. Fern laughed, and I said, "Let's see yours."

"My what?"

"Your stomachache face," I said.

"I don't think I've ever looked in the mirror when I've had a stomachache," Fern said.

"I mean the face you make when you're *faking* a stomachache," I explained.

"Why would I fake a stomachache?" she asked.

"OK, so a headache, a sore throat, whatever." That was me, getting impatient.

Fern looked blank. I looked at her in the mirror, then I looked at her in real life. She was SERIOUS!

At school I performed my brave-sensitive act, concentrating on my posture and sad smile. But Mike Humphrey didn't notice. And he didn't notice the next day or the day after. The situation seemed hopeless. Did I have to cry real tears every single time I wanted to get his attention?

On the last school day of January, I was desperate. I figured that since the Mom story worked the first time, maybe it would work again. So I started acting all anxious and tormented. And actually, since Mom was smoking again, it wasn't that much of a stretch to get worked up about her health.

Finally, after I'd sighed and moaned myself blue

in the face, Mike said, "You OK?"

"It's my mom," I sighed. "She flunked all her medical tests."

"Gee," Mike said, looking a little scared. Maybe he was afraid I was going to start sobbing, or that whatever Mom had was catching.

"We are hoping for the best, though," I said, smiling my brave smile. Mike nodded, looking me right smack in the eye. Then he turned back to his math paper, and I sighed for real. That's *it?* That's all I get for all those moans and countless hours of face-training? Life was so cruel.

Unlike January, which had begun so great with Mom giving up cigarettes and Mike being seated next to me, February stunk from the start. For one thing, Mom was smoking like a chimney, and for another, Mike was torn from my side and shoved way across the room. I had to turn in my seat and peer over two rows of heads just to see him.

And worst of all, Valentine's Day was barreling toward me like a runaway train. I knew that if I couldn't get Mike to like me by then, it would be a seriously bad and deeply unromantic day.

Birdy and I bought the same kind of valentines and went out on my back porch to sign them. She was zipping through the class list at the speed of light. Not me. I agonized over which one would tell Mike how I really felt about him.

At last I chose the kitten one that said, "You are my purrrfect valentine." I asked Birdy what she thought.

"I think it's purrrfect," she said.

"Really?"

"Really."

"Absolutely, positively, a hundred percent sure?"

"Mitzi, I don't think boys read these," Birdy said.

Mike didn't give me a valentine, unless he had stuck it in the wrong locker or something.

I saw my brother dump his backpack full of valentines straight into the kitchen trash without even glancing at them. Why would any girl send *him* one in the first place? Maybe they just looked like valentines—maybe they were really hate mail.

The Sunday after Valentine's Day was one of Dad's concerts at the high school auditorium. "Can we sit in the balcony, PLEASE?" I begged.

Mom turned to Birdy. "Will you behave yourselves?" Birdy nodded, looking straight-faced and trustworthy. "Well, you'd better be good," Mom told us in her sternest teacher voice. "Understand?"

"Yes, yes, yes!" That was both of us.

"OK, I'll see you at intermission," Mom said. Then she ducked out to get her last nicotine fix before the concert.

Birdy and I flew up the stairs. The balcony was empty because we were way earlier than the rest of the audience. That's because Dad always came ages before the concert to drink tea in the greenroom (which wasn't green, but that's what they call the room where the musicians hang out).

We picked the two exact-center seats up front and began deciding whether to be poor, homeless orphan sisters who'd snuck into the auditorium to sleep, or snobby rich girls whom everyone was in a lather to impress.

"If we're the rich girls," I said, "and we hate the music, they'll banish the conductor to a horrid, far-away land of giant spiders."

"One bad word from us and they'll smash the instruments and shred all the musicians' suits and gowns," added Birdy.

I thought of Dad whistling in the mirror, tying his black bow tie, and said, "Let's be the orphans." So we started snoring as the seats began to fill.

When Birdy whispered, "Wake up, sister!" I opened my eyes. The concertmaster played a note, and all the other musicians tuned their instruments to his. Then there was applause as the conductor strutted onstage. "Look!" Birdy said in her most innocent orphan voice. "There's gonna be a show! That man must be the ringmaster. Maybe there'll be clowns and astronauts—I mean acrobats!" That started our giggles.

The conductor raised his baton, and everyone fell silent except us. He jabbed the air and drowned out our laughter with sawing violins and rumbling drums. But the man next to me must have had X-ray hearing. He leaned over to shush us, even though I had practically my whole sweater shoved in my mouth and Birdy was bent over, biting her arm. By intermission we were limp and soggy from trying not to laugh.

"Are you enjoying the concert?" Mom asked us downstairs.

"It was beautiful," Birdy said.

"I knew you'd like Dvořák," Mom said. "He's very dramatic."

I bet Birdy had no idea that Dvořák wrote the music we'd just giggled through, but she nodded seriously. My brother, Les, leaned against the wall, pretending he wasn't with us. Then a man came up and asked Mom if we were her girls.

Mom shot us one of her looks and said, "Yes."

"Well, they were extremely disruptive during the performance," he ratted.

"I'm terribly sorry, sir," Mom said. "It won't happen again."

Les smirked. Nothing made him happier than when I got in trouble.

Mom made me and Birdy apologize to the old grump. Then she marched us outside so she could rant at us and smoke. Birdy chewed on her nails. I peered through the glass doors, wishing the lights would flick on and off for the end of intermission. Then I saw MIKE HUMPHREY!

I yanked the door open to go after him, but Mom barked, "I'm not through with you, young lady!" I had to stay to hear the rest of her lecture. Then she made me and Birdy sit downstairs, on either side of her, for the rest of the concert. I twisted in my seat, trying to spot Mike in the dark, but I couldn't.

Soon the lights would come on and there would be a general mash toward the doors. What if I did see Mike and he saw me—with my MOM? Mom, in all her momness, fit as a fiddle, when she was supposed to be sick! What if he introduced himself? I couldn't introduce Mom as Mom! I'd have to—what? Scream "FIRE"? No, that's illegal and I'd be arrested. Although if I were in jail, I'd never have to explain to Mike why my sick mother was at this concert.

And maybe Mike would come to the prison on visiting day and smuggle me a file in a pineapple upside-down cake. We'd plot my escape in code, using blinks. I'd dig an amazing secret tunnel, and Mike and I would meet outside the gates at exactly midnight. Off we'd run, terrified but thrilled to be together, dodging searchlights with trained killer dogs on our trail!

The music and applause had stopped. Mom was hightailing it up the aisle, in a hurry to get outside and fill her lungs with smoke. Les was shuffling behind her, way too cool to lift his feet off the ground. I grabbed Birdy and called to my mom that we were going backstage. I ran against the tide, dragging Birdy down the aisle with me, onto the stage, and finally behind the curtain.

"Mike Humphrey was in the audience!" I panted.

"So why'd we run away?" Birdy asked.

Hmmm. I'd never had a secret from Birdy before, and I felt lonely having one now. But I couldn't tell her about the sick mom thing *now*, could I? Not after *not* telling her for so long. So instead I said, "I got shy."

Birdy rolled her eyes, as if I were a total dweeb.

When we got to the greenroom, Birdy nudged me. I knew she wanted me to giggle with her about the bald-headed trumpet player, who was busy cleaning the spit out of his instrument. He was a normal color now, but from the balcony we had watched his head turn redder and redder with every note, until we'd been sure he was going to explode. I wasn't interested in the trumpet player anymore, though. All I could think about was Mike Humphrey.

Was Mike a musician as well as a runner? Would he want to be my boyfriend if he knew my dad was in the orchestra? Maybe he'd like free violin lessons! I'd have to pay Dad out of my allowance, but it would be worth it. Mike would come over for his lesson and stay for dinner. Then we'd sneak out for a moonlight stroll. The night-blooming jasmine would fill the air with romantic perfume. Sigh.

# 4
## Cleanliness and the Clone

Birdy started sitting with that Roxy Gold-girl every day on the bus. If I asked Birdy what they talked about, she said, "Nothing." But if I didn't ask, it was all "Roxy this, Roxy that. Roxy thinks blah about blah blah blah."

Birdy's real name was Roberta, and Roxy's real name was Roxanne, so both their names started with *R* and had seven letters. Big deal. And Roxy called Birdy "Bobby," which Birdy adored. She wanted ME to start calling her that, too.

Roxy was a vegetarian, and she thought Birdy should cut her hair. I had medium-length, medium-brown, medium-boring hair and thought Birdy's long black waves were gorgeous. But when I said so, she flicked her hand as if my opinion were a bug on her finger.

We saw an antismoking movie in health class. It started with a list of famous people who had died from smoking. Names rolled by, too fast and too many to read. Then it showed horrid pictures of miserable people. A man with half his face missing tried to say that he wished he had never started smoking. A woman smoked through a hole in her neck. It was entirely gross and it scared me to death about Mom.

But as I was walking out of the room, I found myself right next to Mike! Kids were shoving, and we got pushed really close together. Being so near him made me dizzy, but this was my big chance.

"That's how my mom got sick," I told him.

"What is?"

"She smokes like a brush fire," I added, truthfully.

"Wow!" His wide mouth twisted down. "What's she got?"

"You mean, disease-wise?" I asked. "It's, um, called . . ." My eyes landed on Mike's shirt, which had blue and yellow stripes. "St . . . Stripitis," I stammered. "It's very rare."

I could have kicked myself. *Stripitis?* That

sounded so stupid! What if he looked down at his shirt? He'd know I'd made it up. But his hazel eyes were sympathetic, and the deed was done.

"Don't tell anyone," I whispered. "I don't want pity." I stood tall when I said that. "It'll be our secret, all right?" Then I showed him my brave, sad smile.

As I walked to my next class, I had a little blip in my stomach—maybe guilt, maybe indigestion, maybe just a loose speck of love splashing around in the sea of my crush. Whatever it was, I was pretty sure it was saying that maybe this was not the absolute best way to start things with Mike. But then I remembered the sweetness in his hazel eyes, and, well . . . *Stripitis* could just be another word for smoker's breath, right?

Mom was all wild with excitement at dinner that night. She had gotten a job substitute-teaching for the rest of the year, filling in for a woman who was leaving to have a baby. Mom, who had been looking for a full-time teaching position for months, was thrilled to have gotten at least a semi-permanent job. We all cheered. That is, Dad and I cheered. Les just grunted.

"So I've got to hurry up and quit smoking!" Mom declared.

*Glunk.* I felt her words in my gut. I desperately

wanted her to be a nonsmoker, but her nasty first quit came back to me like a bad-tasting burp.

"When?" I asked, hoping it wasn't anytime soon.

"Friday!" she said, as if announcing a trip to Disneyland. "That gives me a little over three weeks before my job starts."

After supper I called up Birdy. "My mom's quitting again."

"Good," she said. "Our class saw a really gross film today about smoking. Cancer, emphysema, and all that."

"I saw it, too," I said, remembering my conversation with Mike Humphrey. Suddenly my ears were attacked by the ghastly screech of cat yowls and train wrecks—Les was practicing the clarinet. "I'M COMING OVER!" I yelled into the phone.

I walked into Birdy's room, and my eyeballs spronged out of my head. Her hair was short, short, short!

"Like it?" Birdy asked, giving her head a bouncy shake like a girl on a shampoo commercial.

"Well, it's different," I hedged. She looked like a dark-haired version of her mother, but that would have been mean to say. "Does it feel strange?"

"My neck is cold," Birdy laughed. "And I keep going like this to push my hair back, but there's nothing to push!"

Birdy handed me a hammer and told me to bash a few tiles for the mosaic she was working on. She said it would make me feel better. I wasn't sure if she meant about her new haircut or about Mom's next quit.

We decided we were artists in ancient Greece who'd been brought by chariot to design a mosaic mural for the Emperor. "The Emperor's really cute, and he's looking for a new queen," Birdy said. "But we don't know that yet."

"What happened to the old queen?" I asked.

"She designed an ugly mural," Birdy said. "She'd told the Emperor she was an artist, but it was a lie."

"So he killed her?"

"No, I think he just banished her. Maybe he did kill her. No one knows for sure."

I smashed three yellow tiles to dust. "Are these pieces too small?" I asked.

Birdy snatched the hammer out of my hand. "Mitzi, I know your mom was crabby last time," she said. "But maybe it's easier the second time, and you want her to quit, right?"

"Right," I grumbled, "but I think the Emperor's wife is called an empress, not a queen. And I don't want to marry him."

"Didn't I tell you who the Emperor is?" Birdy asked. "Mike Humpty!"

"HUMPHREY, not HUMPTY!" I yelled, "His name's MIKE HUMPHREY!"

Tuesday, nothing. Wednesday, nothing. But Thursday Mike said "Hi" to me. The "Hi" happened because I was leaning on his locker before class, humming. Actually, it was a you're-in-my-way-and-I-gotta-open-my-locker kind of "Hi," but it was better than nothing.

I'd hoped my hum would start a musical conversation that would lead to me mentioning that my dad was a musician. But then I realized that standing around humming happily, with my mom so deathly ill, was very tacky. So I just got out of his way and knocked right into Ms. Cook, the principal. She spilled her coffee, HOT coffee, on my shirt. I don't know if Mike saw it. I did *not* turn around to check.

At Girls' After-School, Fern asked what the blob was on my shirt. I told her it was a map of Africa for a school project. I was just kidding, but she studied my stain seriously and said it needed more of a tail at the bottom.

Then it was Friday, my mom's quit day. I came home from school and tiptoed around, thinking she was in her room sulking. But then she called to me from deep within her closet. Clothes were flying out.

"What are you doing?" I asked.

"I'm washing out the smoke stink," Mom said, backing out of her closet and talking fast. "I'm cleaning my clothes, the rugs, the curtains. Our home will be healthful and wholesome!"

"Don't forget the car," I said. "It totally reeks."

Mom scooped up an armload of clothing and headed for the laundry room, leaving a trail of underwear behind her. After shoving in a load, she started wiping the top of the washing machine and the walls around it. Then she was down on the floor, poking at ancient lint balls between the washer and dryer. "Let's do the windows next," she said.

"Not me," I said. "I gotta go to Birdy's."

"But Mitzi," Mom whined, "I need you to help me take out the screens and hose them down, and then scrub the windows!"

I suddenly noticed the fish tank was dazzlingly clean, the water sparkling. I wondered if she had scoured the fish themselves. "I gotta go study for my math test," I explained. "Birdy's going to help me." Mom looked crushed. "I'll help with the screens on the weekend," I promised and bolted out the door.

★ ★ ★

Birdy jumped as if I'd caught her stealing something. "You should call before you come over," she said, tossing her short hair.

"Huh?" That was me, confused.

"Well, like in case I have company or something," Birdy said. I must have looked blank because then Birdy added, "No big deal. I just think you should call first."

I stood around feeling weird until Birdy asked if I wanted to help with her weaving. I sat down and started trying to untangle a clot of yarn. But Birdy soon snatched it away, saying, "Hey! You're shredding it to bits." She told me to sort by color instead. "Nonviolently, please," she said.

After a while I told her about my mom's cleanliness quit.

Birdy waved her hands in front of my face. "It must be quitting season. I quit biting my nails, see?" Her fingernails were still stubby, but when I looked closely, I did see maybe a trace of nail growing.

"Was that Roxy's idea?" I asked.

Birdy rolled her eyes. "NO, it was NOT Roxy's idea. I'm just too old for having ugly hands." I didn't think Birdy's hands were ugly. They just looked like Birdy's hands.

"Mitzi, you're supposed to say congratulations or something."

"Congratulations or something," I said.

"And guess what," Birdy said. "Todd Ullah asked Roxy to be his girlfriend."

"Wow!" I gasped. I couldn't help being impressed. Everyone loved Todd Ullah. Everyone.

"And you know what else?"

"What?"

"Roxy told him she had to THINK about it!"

I bit back a second "Wow!" before it could slip out. But wouldn't Birdy "Wow!" herself green if Mike Humphrey asked me to be *his* girlfriend? "He brought flowers and candy," I'd explain modestly. "Then he got down on one knee and begged!"

On Monday Mike was standing alone against the fence before school. Of course I was dying for him to know that I was willing to be his girlfriend, but I figured I better just start with another "Hi."

"How's your mother?" he asked, looking cute, cute, cute.

"She's doing the best she can," I said.

"So is she home now or in the hospital or what?" he asked.

"The hospital," I said, while my inside voice was screaming, "THIS IS A CONVERSATION! A LONG ONE!"

"Which one?"

"Which one what?" I asked. "Oh, which hospital? Um . . ." I said the first thing that popped into my head. "Seventh-Day Adventist."

"Hey, my mom works there!" Mike smiled an eighth of his fabulous smile at me. "She's a nurse. I could have her check on your mom. Maybe sneak her an extra Jell-O!"

Panic. "NO!" I said. "My mother is very, um . . . shy. Really, terribly shy. She'd be so embarrassed if anyone she knew, or, um, I mean anyone who knew anyone she knew, saw her. And Jell-O gives her gas. But thanks anyway."

"Oh," he said.

I searched desperately for a way to get him off the subject of my mom. I thought about telling him that I'd seen him at the concert, but I caught myself just in time. After all, how could I be going to concerts if I was always at the hospital? What kind of future girlfriend would abandon her sick mother to go to a concert?

Before I could think of anything else to say, Mike said, "See ya!" and walked away. I squinted into the sun, watching him leave. He had a funny walk—a wonderfully funny walk, even if it was in the wrong direction (away from me). I sighed. This was NOT going well.

About two hours later I was standing in front of

my composition class reading my oral report when I suddenly thought, Did I tell Mike Humphrey that Jell-O gives my mom GAS? No, I *couldn't* have, could I?! Did I?!

"Is something wrong, Mitzi?" my teacher asked.

"YES!" I wanted to say. "EVERYTHING IS TOTALLY, COMPLETELY WRONG!" But instead I made myself keep reading. After all, the show must go on! I was a true performer. I belonged on the stage—no, in the movies. I could see it all now. Rejected in my youth because of a crude comment I once made, I turn to acting and become an unbelievably rich celebrity. My birthday becomes a national holiday. My picture is on a stamp.

Then, when I'm old, I'm still amazingly talented and beautiful and my fans love me as much as ever, but it's time for me to retire. My doctors insist. So, who comes knocking on my dressing room door? None other than that long-ago heartbreaker from Ms. London's homeroom—Mike Humphrey! He's old, too, but still really cute. He tells me he's always loved me, and I die happy in his arms. Well, not *that* happy. I'm dead after all. If that's not already a movie, it should be. Starring ME.

Mom lasted four or five days on the cleanliness quit. By then her hands were chapped from hours in soapy water, and the house was spotless. My brother, who was only comfortable when surrounded by filth, complained that he couldn't find anything in his room anymore. He got a lock for his door.

With Mom smoking and back to normal, Birdy started coming over again. One night my mom invited her to stay for dinner. Birdy asked what we were having.

"Lasagna."

"With meat?" Birdy asked.

"There's ground turkey in the sauce," answered my mom.

"No thanks," Birdy said. "I'm a vegetarian."

Oh no! I thought. Birdy's becoming a short-haired, nail-growing, vegetarian ROXY CLONE!

# 5
# Fitness and Freckles

It took a while for my mom to get up her courage for quit number three. "I can't just jump into it," she explained, "without recovering from the last one." But when she had only a week and a half left before her job started, she began the vigorous-exercise quit.

"The Y Girls' After-School mother-daughter camping weekend is coming up," I reminded her on the second day of her quit.

"How could I possibly think about that without a cigarette?" she grunted, touching her toes. I knew better than to answer that question. I think about everything without a cigarette. It can be done by most people. Normal moms think with-out cigarettes, and what they think about is their *kids*—what they want and need. But my mom only thought about her quits and herself. The grunt-and-sweat quit, like the clean-machine and the mean-in-bed quits, was taking over her life, and I was mighty sick of it.

When I got home from school, Mom nabbed me and made me do a workout video with her. She never made Les work out with her. She never made Les do anything.

I hated the lady on the video, who kept yelling, "SWEAT!"

"She's a bully," I said. "How can you stand her?"

"I can't," Mom sputtered. "But just do what she says. The best part is turning it off when we're done. You'll see (*pant, pant*), it feels great." But I didn't wait to find out.

"TRAITOR!" Mom yelled after me as I snuck out of the room.

After school the next day, Mom dragged me to the high school track to go jogging.

"Mom," I said, "don't you have a girlfriend you could do this with?"

"Don't be lazy, Mitzi," she huffed as she stretched out. "It will do you a world of good to start exer-cising while you're young. You'll thank me for this someday. I only wish my mother had encouraged me to be more active."

I tried to imagine my grandma in a jogging suit. It made me giggle. Just then a blur of human motion streaked past us, and my knees went to jelly. It was Mike Humphrey.

"C'mon, Mitzi!" Mom said and sprinted off. Well, not exactly *sprinted*—more like walked fast with extra arm flinging. I watched Mike get farther and farther ahead, then come around the track behind us. I tried to think of something runnerish to call out to him, but my mind was a blank.

*Zip!* He passed us. Well, even if I couldn't think of something sporty to say, at least he would see me running and know we had a lot in common. But what if he thought this woman I was running with was my MOTHER? I could introduce her as my coach, but how would I explain that to *Mom*?

It didn't matter, though, because by the time we lugged ourselves around the track, Mike had passed us three times without even glancing in my direction. Then he left. My feet hurt.

I went up to him the next day and said, "I saw you at the track yesterday. I was jogging with my AUNT."

He looked right past me and said, "Oh."

I turned around to see what he was looking at.

It was a girl in our class named Vanessa. Hmmm, I thought, Vanessa.

Mom announced that she felt brave enough to go on the Y Girls' After-School mother-daughter camping trip with me after all. Dad called her heroic, as if we were going to climb Mount Everest barefoot.

Mom could hardly pack because of the nicotine withdrawal symptom *trouble concentrating*.

Mom: "We should probably bring swimsuits in case there's a pool."

Me: "We did."

Mom: "Did what?"

Me: "Pack bathing suits."

Mom: "Good idea, Mitzi! Let's bring our suits in case there's a pool!"

On the way to meet the bus, Mom demonstrated her other favorite symptom, *irritability,* by honking at every single car on the road. "Excuse me, but I'm USING this lane!" she yelled at one car. "The GAS pedal is the one on the RIGHT side!" she yelled at another.

When we pulled into the Y parking lot, I noticed a woman near the heap of duffel bags—*smoking.* Mom smiled the first real smile I'd seen on her face for days and said, "Mitzi, do you see what I see?"

Then she screeched out of the parking lot and zoomed to the nearest Quick Mart. "There's no way I could spend a weekend with that woman smoking in my face," Mom quickly explained. "I'm sure I'd bum a cigarette from her, and then another one. Mooching is rude, you know, especially with the price of cigarettes these days."

Mom jumped from the car and ran into the store singing, "Neither a borrower nor a lender be!"

I listened to the car pinging its "Hey, you forgot your key!" bell, and I sat there feeling guilty. I was glad Mom had decided to smoke. Even if it meant she was getting heart disease and her lungs were filling up with deadly gunk, at least we'd have fun camping.

And we did have fun, until a girl who must go to the Y on a different day than me introduced herself and her mother as Nina and Gloria HUMPHREY! There was no mistaking the wide mouths on those two. I hustled my mom away, my heart beating the buttons loose on my shirt. And from then on, the trip was pure squirm.

I did everything I could to keep my mom away from Mike's mom, but they kept finding each other. Every time I blinked, they were together again. At one point, when Fern cornered me and began flapping her lips, Mom slipped out of sight.

I fidgeted in a hurry-up kind of way, but Fern's story wouldn't end. Finally I said I had to go to the bathroom and raced off to hunt down my mom.

And, of course, because this is just how life is, I found her yucking it up with Mike's mom at the campfire as if they were best friends. If I'd wanted the two mothers to like each other, they probably would have become instant enemies.

I swatted Mom's back, screaming that there was a giant spider on her. "I think it's a black widow!" That broke up their conversation nicely. But what if it was already too late? It was entirely possible that Mom had already invited Mrs. Humphrey and her whole widemouthed family over for dinner. Mom was forever dragging new people home so Dad could burn food for them on his grill.

*Dingdong,* the doorbell would ring. "Mitzi, the Humphreys are here," I imagined Dad calling. I'd float gracefully downstairs. My hair wouldn't be frizzing and I'd be wearing something much prettier than anything I actually own. Mike would look up at me. Something would click in his mind. A click of love. But then, my mother would come in. Mike would see her looking as healthy as a horse. He'd look at me—he'd look at Mom. Then there'd be another click, a click of hate. He'd run from my house, from my life, forever.

I wished, wished, wished we'd never come on this stupid camping trip!

And the other smoking woman, the one we'd seen by the duffel bags, must have just been dropping someone off because we never saw her again. So, as always, my mother was the only smoker.

It was humiliating. Whenever Mom lit up, people looked at her as if she were picking her nose. And they fanned the air when they walked past her.

"Doesn't your mom know that smoking is bad for her?" Fern asked me.

"I think a couple of people may have mentioned it," I replied. But Fern, ever the do-gooder Scout, decided to inform my mom about the perils of smoking. Mom replied as she did to anyone who dared to question her smoking. She glared her frosty mind-your-own-business glare and froze Fern to the spot. Icicles formed in Fern's hair.

The last misery to endure was the bus ride home. I made Mom sit in the back with me, even though all the other moms were sitting together up front. I told her I felt woozy. She opened the window as far as she could and watched me with concern.

"Maybe it's the bus fumes," Fern suggested.

My brother moaned when I walked in the door. "I was hoping you'd left for that northern Alaska boarding school for terminal losers," he said. But I was so glad to be home-sweet-home that I didn't even bother fighting with him.

I headed straight for Birdy's. I had missed her terribly whenever I'd remembered to. It was time to tell her about the whole Mike thing. I couldn't STAND being in it alone anymore, especially if I was going to get caught. But then I started wondering how Birdy would react. Would she think I was awful and hate me? Or would she think I was stupid and treat me like a baby?

I stopped and sat on the front steps of the church. I broke into a sweat just thinking about the mess I'd gotten myself into. If only I could rewind and erase everything since January tenth, 9:48 A.M. This time, when Mike asked if I was OK, I'd say, "Something's in my eye." He'd flick the eyelash away with his finger. Then he'd notice that I have hazel eyes like his. Harps would play, doves would fly. He'd wear that lucky eyelash in a silver locket around his neck forever. We'd be M & M, Mitzi and Mike, for all eternity. Sigh.

But it was too late for that. I decided to take my chances with Birdy. I got to my feet and dusted off my butt. I marched across the lawn, through Birdy's kitchen door, and straight upstairs. Her bedroom door was shut, but even if I'd thought to knock,

Birdy wouldn't have heard me over Milt's TV. I threw open the door, and there were Birdy and ROXY. They were hunched in front of Birdy's mirror, putting on lipstick.

I said, "Oh."

Birdy leaped up, but it was definitely NOT a leap of joy. I'd never noticed before how really ugly her freckles got when she blushed.

## Lice
## and Gruel

By morning I was ready to forgive and forget. As Birdy and I walked to the bus, I asked her if she wanted to ride bikes after school.

"I can't. Roxy's coming over."

*Again?* "So you're really good friends now?" I asked, hoping she'd say something like, "No, not really." But instead, she said, "Yeah."

I nodded, acting as casual as I could. "So, did she decide to be Todd Ullah's girlfriend?"

"Yeah."

The bus pulled up. Roxy had saved Birdy a seat. I sat next to Fern. I talked loudly to her and laughed a lot, but I don't think Birdy noticed. She probably wouldn't have been jealous even if she had noticed. She'd probably have been RELIEVED!

After school, Roxy and Birdy got off the bus together and walked home as if they were the only two girls on Earth. I trailed behind, alone. I was sure glad I hadn't told Birdy about the whole Mike Humphrey–Stripitis thing. I could imagine her snickering about it with Roxy Gold-creep.

When I got home, my mom was digging around in her cactus bed. I hated cactuses. I thought they were ugly and mean, and I wished Mom would grow flowers like a normal person. But she said she preferred cactuses because they weren't greedy for water and they made good watchdogs. I guess she thought they'd shred the burglars to death.

"Mom," I said, "Birdy has a new best friend. Her name's ROXY."

Mom straightened up. I was expecting her to say, "Birdy may have a new friend, but certainly not a new BEST friend! You'll always be Birdy's BEST friend!" But instead she said, "And you hate Roxy and wish she'd shrivel up and blow away?"

"Well, I don't know if I HATE her," I said. "Well, yeah, I guess I hate her."

"I bet you hate Birdy a little, too, right?"

"She's being a total zit about the whole thing.

They just walked home from the bus together and didn't say one word to me."

Mom smiled a weird smile.

"It's not funny," I said.

"No, of course not," she said, pulling a pack of cigarettes out of her shirt pocket. "It's not funny, but it's so completely predictable that it's *almost* funny. Like baby teeth falling out. Like hair growing in armpits."

I didn't say anything. There were streaks of blood on her arms from her ungrateful cactuses. I watched her shake a cigarette out of her pack and light it. She had only one week left to smoke her guts out, and she was making the most of it.

"Do you remember my best friend, Ethel?" Mom asked, exhaling a huge gush of smoke.

"No, who's Ethel?"

"That's exactly my point, Mitzi. Ethel was my dearest friend. We were inseparable. We loved the same books, the same songs, and the same movie stars. We even wore the same size. When I needed bigger shoes, so did she. And now my own daughter doesn't know who Ethel is. Ethel probably doesn't even know I have a daughter."

"Why did you stop being friends?" I asked.

Mom shrugged. "I can't remember. But the point is . . . well, I don't know what the point is, exactly, but the *truth* is that not all friendships last forever. I'm sorry, Mitzi," she said and gave me a hug, trying not to drop ashes on my sleeve. "By the way, I ran into one of the women from our camping trip today at the market, and she . . ."

"WHICH ONE?" I yelped. "Don't talk to any of those women!"

Mom raised her eyebrows. I tried to sound calm. "After-School mothers have to stay away from each other. It's in the YWCA rule book," I explained. "I can show you where it's written."

"I'd like to see that," Mom said.

"We are supposed to make friends by OUR-SELVES," I stammered. "And it's cheating if our families get chummy." Even I knew that was pretty lame. "Which mother was it, though?" I asked.

"I don't remember her name," Mom said, looking at me with squinty eyes. "But she told me that several girls came home from the trip with head lice and I should check your hair for nits."

"Oh," I said, relieved. Then her words sunk in. "HEAD LICE? EEEW!" And I ran around scratching my head and screaming.

Mom sat me under her desk lamp and searched through my hair. "You had lice when you were in preschool," she said. "Remember? We had to quarantine your stuffed animals."

I cringed. *Lice!* What if Mike found out? Oh wait! Maybe his sister was one of the girls who got them, so he'd think it was OK. No, that was going too far. Even if he was ultra-pals with his sister, he'd still be grossed out.

"If I were a mother chimp," Mom said, "I'd pick out your bugs and eat them. Oh! Here's a tasty-looking one!"

"YOU FOUND ONE?" I shrieked.

"Just kidding," Mom said.

Birdy called after dinner and asked if I wanted to come over. I grabbed my jacket and raced across the church lawn. I'd meant to crab about how mean she'd been to me, but I was so glad she called that I didn't say a word.

Birdy was doing a sand painting, even though she knew that sand, sandpaper, any of that scritchy stuff, always gave me the shivers. I figured it was Roxy's idea.

I told Birdy about the head-lice scare, and she made me sit across the room from her. As she poured the sand, we pretended that I was watching it trickle through an hourglass while she tried to finish her work in time so we could get our weekly bowl of gruel.

The evil headmistress of our northern Alaskan

boarding school sold Birdy's sand paintings for a fortune. But did *we* ever see a nickel of that money? No. We had head lice and were given nothing to eat but gruel. Nonetheless, we loved our gruel.

When it was time for me to go home, I asked the question that had been on my mind. "Do you do stuff like this with Roxy?"

"Stuff like what?"

"Like boarding school, like orphans. You know what I mean, Birdy."

"I told you, Mitzi, I'm not BIRDY anymore, I'm BOBBY!" I wondered if that was a yes or a no, but I let it drop.

I wore my green shirt on St. Patrick's Day. I knew that was cheating because most of the kids and even the teachers would be wearing green, too, so it wouldn't really count as a cosmic connection with Mike. Would it? The answer was no. I wore green, Mike wore green, and nothing happened.

That Saturday I went with Mom to help her set up her classroom. The pregnant teacher had left, and Mom was taking over the class on Monday. She was very excited and still smoking. "Well, how could I quit NOW, with all of these life changes to adjust to?" she asked.

Her new school was older and darker than my school. The desks were splintery wood instead of that plasticky smooth stuff our desks were made of.

"It's totally depressing in here," I said.

"Well, we're here to cheer it up," said Mom.

We began tearing curled, faded papers off the walls and shoving them in the trash. While we were working, Mom asked me about Birdy.

"It's like I'm her secret, invisible friend and she'll only hang around with me when no one else is around," I explained. "It's strange."

My mom nodded. "And have *you* been shopping around for a new best friend?"

"Not really. I'm waiting for Birdy to turn back into Birdy."

"That might not happen, you know. Come on outside," she said, grabbing her purse. I knew what that meant.

"You said you weren't going to smoke anywhere near the new school, Mom."

"It's Saturday. Weekends don't count."

We went behind the building to the playground, but there were kids there. We walked all the way around the school, but no place looked safe to her. "If you ever smoke, I'll kill you," Mom said, leading me to her car. We rolled down the windows. She lit up and took a huge drag on her cigarette.

Then another car pulled into the parking lot, and Mom ducked down under the dashboard to exhale.

I said, "Mom, this is pretty crazy you know."

"Hmmph," was her reply.

It turned out that while I was helping Mom clean her classroom and sneak around to smoke, Birdy and Roxy Gold-spit went ice-skating. At the bus stop Monday morning, Birdy told me that they had met Todd Ullah and his friend Nathan at the ice rink, where they all had a fabulous, terrifically hilarious time. She said they might go skating again next weekend. Needless to say, she did not invite me along.

"Since when are you such a skater?" I asked.

"Oh, Mitzi," Birdy said. "Don't be so naive. It's not about skating!"

"I know that," I said. Then, when I could breathe normally, I said, "So what's this Nathan guy like? Is he in your class?"

"He goes to a whole different school!" Birdy said, as if going to a different school was exotic, mysterious, and romantic. "He goes to Taft."

"My mom's teaching at Kennedy," I said. "Their desks are splintery and all gouged up with initials."

"I wonder if Nathan will carve my initials in his desk," Birdy sighed.

# 7
## Girl Talk and a Curse

"Hey, Worm," my brother said, "M.H. called to talk to you."

"WHAT?"

"He told me to tell you to call him right back. Says he's madly in love with you."

First my stomach jumped up. Then it slammed down.

"April Fools'," Les laughed and smacked me on the back of my head. Everyone is annoying on April Fools' Day, but Les is beyond obnoxious.

"MOM!" I yelled. "Les just hit me and he's been reading my diary!"

"Don't fight," came Mom's feeble reply. "Please,

kids, I have a splitting headache." She was slumped in a chair, looking like overcooked pasta.

Dad was setting up take-out chicken for dinner. We had been having mostly take-out since Mom started her teaching job. She came home exhausted every day, usually with a headache. She blamed it on a kid in her class named Jake. Jake, she said, was going to be an ax murderer—or worse. Mom told us stories about Jake's evil deeds every night at dinner, if she wasn't too tired to speak.

In the meantime, Mike had been absent from school for two days. Probably his dad was a bank robber running from the law. After the holdup he had told Mike, "Get yer things, boy, and make it snappy. We're outta here!" A taxi had then picked them up—no, a shiny black getaway car, waiting with the motor running. "To the airport," Mike's dad had grunted at the driver, "and step on it!"

But as they'd passed my house, Mike made his dad stop so he could climb up to my window and whisper, "Mitzi, I'll never forget you!" Then he was gone, but his words still rattled my mini-blinds. Curtains stirring would be much more romantic than mini-blinds clinking, but I didn't really think I could ask Mom for curtains when she was in such a bad Jake-mood.

At Girls' After-School, I happened to mention to my so-called friend Fern that I thought Mike Humphrey liked me.

"No, I don't think so," Fern said, as if we were talking about something of no importance. "His sister Nina told me that Mike calls Vanessa Cardin every night to say goodnight."

"That's a lie!" I said.

"I don't lie," Fern huffed. "I'm a Girl Scout."

That Thursday Mike was back at school. Turns out he'd had an ear infection. It's hard to feel totally romantic about an ear infection. But I was glad he was back. I ran after him in the hall, figuring it was time to cry again. Maybe he'd put his arms around me and let me sob on his shoulder. The thought made my knees wiggly.

Mike smiled a fraction of his smile and asked, "What's the name of your mom's disease again?"

My mind went blank. *Shirtitis?* No, that wasn't right. I knew it had to do with his shirt, but what? Panic! Panic! It was a color or a pattern, right? *Blueitis? Plaiditis?* While I stood there like a dope, my tongue searching my mouth for the right word, Vanessa appeared at Mike's side. He turned to beam his megawatt smile at her without even waiting to hear my answer! Life is so totally unfair.

I kept an eye on Vanessa the rest of the day. I knew Fern's story about the goodnight phone calls had to be total, one hundred percent garbage, but there was *something* going on. How grotesque, I thought, deep in self-pity.

When I finally remembered the word *Stripitis*, I wrote it ten times in my notebook. I'd never let myself forget *that* word again!

I was a little mad at Fern for saying that Mike called Vanessa every night, because it felt like Fern had made it true just by saying it. I avoided her at the Y and stopped sitting with her on the bus, but she didn't seem to notice—she even asked me if I wanted to come over to her house. I decided to tell her I couldn't because I'd gotten a job working after school. Fern laughed as if I was joking.

I noticed that Mom was starting to look a little stringy. She had bags under her eyes now and limp hair. She dragged home from school each day and slumped in a chair, filling ashtrays with butts. The fish tank was starting to cloud up with green slime. The fish looked concerned.

Mom said Jake was getting worse. He stole kids' lunches and flushed them down the toilet, ruining the plumbing. He spit in the other kids' desks. He wrote swearwords on the board. Mom said she was sure that the last teacher had just pretended to be pregnant to get away from him. She said her entire school day was spent policing Jake.

My family's dinner conversations became all about Jake. Les suggested strangling him, and my mother nodded as if she were actually considering it. No one mentioned quitting smoking, not at a time like this.

Meanwhile, Mom had one cold after another. She said her whole class was a petri dish of infectious diseases. All of her students smeared their drippy noses on her.

Mom brought one of the colds home to share with me. We spent a day together in her bed, napping and sneezing. Neither one of us had good aim, so there were more wads of tissue around the wastebasket than in it. Dad delivered meals to our door and said we reminded him of when I was a baby and Mom was always carting me off to her bed to cuddle with.

"Mom, did you ever like a boy?" I asked.

"Very funny," she said.

"I mean before Dad. When you were my age."

"Sure, plenty of them," she said, bunching her pillow under her head.

"Did they like you back?"

"Sometimes. Why? Do you like someone?"

I half nodded, half shrugged.

"Is he nice?"

"I dunno," I said. "I *think* so."

"Is he funny? Funny is important."

I thought about that.

"Smart?" Mom asked.

I scooted deeper into the blankets.

"Does he like you back?"

I pulled the blanket over my head, and Mom laughed.

"I can hardly get him to notice me, and I've tried EVERYTHING!" I mumbled from underneath the blanket.

Then Mom ducked under the blanket with me and said, "It's a great mystery what boys notice and what they don't. I once had a horrible crush on a boy named Alan Schneider. He wouldn't give me the time of day, so one day I tripped him. His books went flying, and he sprained his wrist and started to howl, and I got sent to the office. He had to miss an important soccer game because of his arm, and his parents wanted to sue my parents." Mom shivered. "Here it is almost thirty years later, and it *still* embarrasses me to think about it."

I giggled.

"So," Mom continued, "whatever you do, don't trip him!"

My dad's voice came from outside our blanket tent. "That's your romantic advice to our daughter? 'Don't trip him?' What ever happened to, 'Just be yourself'?"

Mom and I squealed and poked our heads out. "Hey! No eavesdropping on girl talk allowed!" Mom shouted.

The next morning I felt well enough to go back to school, but Mom didn't. She stayed home again, feeling awful and blowing her red nose. The next day, too.

Mom's cough got so bad that it kept me awake at night. At first all that hacking and honking just got on my nerves, but then it turned scary when my anti-medical mother actually made a doctor's appointment. That's when I realized that she had begun to look just the way I'd imagined a person with Stripitis looking!

I got shaky. What if my lie had caused her to get sick? I pictured a scraggly-haired witch doctor telling my mom, "This is no common illness. This is the sign of a CURSE!" She grabs Mom's hands in her leathery palms and says, "Someone near and dear to you is responsible for this." Then she raises her spooky yellow eyes and looks right at ME.

★ ★ ★

Mom picked me up from school to go to the doctor with her. She was still smoking even though she was sick. *(Puff, puff. Hack, hack, hack.)*

"Mom, maybe you shouldn't smoke when you're coughing."

"You're absolutely right, Mitzi," she said, lighting another one.

We waited and waited in the waiting room. Mom ducked outside once to smoke while I waited for her name to be called. When she came back, I was ready to confess the whole Stripitis story. Not that I really thought I'd caused her to be sick, but I decided I had to tell her—just in case. And what was the worst thing that could happen if I told her about my lie? She could laugh at me, tease me, tell my dad and everyone else. Or she could get mad, I supposed, and punish me, throw me out of the house, maybe even disown me.

But I had to take my chances.

I watched her leaf through a magazine way too fast to be reading the words. Her foot was tapping.

I began, "Mom?"

"Hmmm?" She flipped more pages and then blew her nose.

"Mom, did you ever tell a fib?"

"No, never *(hack, hack)*. Well, *that's* a fib. So I guess I have. Little ones."

"Well, did you, um . . . ever tell a little one that sort of GREW?"

She looked up from her magazine. "Grew?"

"Sandy Burk?" the nurse at the door said. Mom sprang to her feet, tossing her magazine into my lap.

"Wait here," she said and coughed.

About fifty hours later, Mom came out clutching little sample bottles of medicine. She shoved them all in my hands so she could rummage in her purse for her cigarettes and keys.

"It's bronchitis," she said. "Gotta take antibiotics and rest. How am I supposed to rest? A class full of kids to teach, *Jake,* and a house to run—rest when?"

BRONCHITIS! I thought. Hooray! Bronchitis is a wonderful thing. Even *I've* had it. Mom was just plain everyday sick, and my lie had nothing to do with it. Phew! Thank goodness I hadn't spilled the beans.

My mother was soon feeling better, but I wondered if I'd done permanent damage to my own soul by telling the whole Stripitis lie. Not that it was an out-and-out *absolute* lie. It was more like a "stretcher." That was what Birdy's dad, Milt, called stretching the truth, like it was pizza cheese or chewing gum. And here's why this one was just a stretcher. Number one: Mom really did smoke, and everyone knows smoking makes you deathly ill.

So maybe I was a bit early with the diagnosis, but it wasn't coming totally out of nowhere. And number two: She *was* sick now, double sick—there was the bronchitis, plus she was sick over Jake.

Birdy was sick of hearing about Jake, too. She thought my mother was too hard on him. "He probably just needs love and kindness," she said. "He's only a little first-grader, after all."

"That's not the point," I told her. "I don't care about Jake. I care about what a mess he's making out of my mom."

"Your mom chose to be a teacher," Birdy said, not looking up from her nail polishing.

"Yeah, but she's totally obsessed with this kid. She doesn't even ASK me about MY day."

"Oh, so it's not poor little Jake or even your own mother you're worried about. It's YOURSELF."

Something about the way Birdy said that made it impossible for me to say, "You bet it's me I'm worried about! Roxy has you, Vanessa has Mike, and now some first-grade squirt has my mother. Who has ME? No one, that's who." But instead I asked Birdy if her mom knew she was going skating with boys.

"She sorta knows," Birdy said, "but don't tell her."

"I won't, Birdy," I promised.

"I told you, I don't want you calling me that anymore. I'm Bobby now."

"Sorry, BOBBY," I sneered. Birdy pretended not to notice.

"Has Mike Higgins paid any attention to you yet?" she asked, blowing on her wet nails.

"Humphrey. Mike HUMPHREY!"

"Whatever."

"Yes, BONNIE, Mike Humphrey pays all kinds of attention to me," I said. "We talk constantly!"

"Can you keep a secret?" Birdy asked, starting on her other hand.

"What secret?"

"Just don't tell anyone," Birdy said.

I took a guess. "You and what's-his-name from Taft are together?"

"Who told you?" Birdy gasped.

"Everyone knows," I lied. Then I turned right around and went home.

# 8
## Ick and the Cure

I didn't have to look very far for Mom. She was lying on the couch with a soggy washcloth on her forehead. Another Jake headache, of course. She did not look like she was in the mood to hear about my problems. So I followed the sound of Mozart to my dad's music room. He was playing his violin, staring out the window.

"Why do you always practice standing up?" I asked him. "You sit down at the concerts."

Dad didn't seem to hear my question, but I wasn't surprised. He always goes into a sort of trance when he plays. Eventually, though, he stopped playing and bent over to peer at me as if he was trying to figure out who I was. "By your age, you know, Mozart had composed several sonatas," he told me for the hundredth time.

"By YOUR age, he was dead," I said.

I hadn't meant it to be funny, but Dad cracked up. When he regained control of himself, I told him that Birdy wasn't Birdy anymore. "She wants to be called BOBBY. It's her friend ROXY'S idea."

"Well, Mitzi, maybe we need to go out for ice cream." That was my father's solution for everything. A scoop of mint chocolate chip for him and strawberry swirl for me.

"I wanted a nickname when I was younger," he told me between licks of his cone. "Nicknames were hip. Nicknames meant you were part of a crowd. Uncle Morris had friends called Jazz Man and Buck. His friends were infinitely cooler than me and my little pals."

"Birdy IS a nickname," I reminded him.

"Yeah, but it's a baby one," he said. "You named her that when you were two years old because you couldn't say Roberta."

"So?"

"So Uncle Morris named me Ick because he couldn't say Rick," Dad said. "My folks thought it was funny. Ha ha. Do you think I wanted to carry the name Ick around with me my whole life?"

"Birdy doesn't sound as stupid as Ick," I said.

"But it's still a baby nickname." Dad pointed to a melting drip of my cone and said, "Jazz Man got his nickname because he was a jazz musician—very cool, snapping his fingers to the music in his head. Can't you just picture him wearing black, his eyes closed, wailing on a sax?"

"So how would you picture a girl called Bobby?" I asked.

"Cute, probably, and fun."

"Whose side are you on?" I asked him.

"Your side, kid," Dad said, touching his ice cream cone to mine. "But the world—well, is the world."

Then it was spring break. My brother went off to band camp for the week to torment the other campers with his bloodcurdling clarinet playing. Bad for them—great for me. And Roxy went on vacation with her family.

"What about Nathan?" I asked Birdy. "Did he leave town, too?"

Birdy said, "No."

"Does that mean you'll be going skating with him and stuff all vacation?"

"I don't think so." Birdy sounded puzzled.

I'd meant to be much too busy for Birdy when and if she called me. But I wasn't busy, and I was glad to have her all to myself again, even if it was temporary. I wondered if she was my bad habit. Was this how smoking felt for my mom—liking something even though it hurt her?

Out of the blue, Mom told me she'd signed up for a group-quit at the hospital. "Which hospital?" I asked, fear twisting my gut.

"Seventh-Day Adventist," she said.

I knew it. How could life be so cruel? "Mom, you can't go there!" I blurted. "We're not Seventh-Day Adventists!"

"That doesn't matter, silly," she said.

"Well, they might try to convert you or something. And I hear it's a terrible place, really!"

"Mitzi, I'm getting the distinct impression that you do NOT want me to join this support group. Why would that be?"

For one tiny smidgen of a microsecond, I almost thought about telling Mom the truth, but where would that get me, besides grounded for life? So instead I said, "Well, um, I'm not supposed to tell, but, they have rats at Seventh-Day."

Mom blew a stream of smoke at the ceiling and looked down at me. "Go on," she said.

"And these rats, um, carry the plague! For real. Fern, my friend from Girls' After-School, knows a kid who went there for just a broken arm and then got bit by one of the rats and died. Died to death."

Mom raised her eyebrows. "Your friend Fern has a rich imagination," she said.

"It's the absolute truth! Fern would never lie. She's a Girl Scout. The hospital is trying to hush it up. That's why you haven't heard about it."

"In that case, I'll be scrupulously careful to avoid all rats," Mom said, squinting at me.

So, heedless of my warnings, Mom went to the hospital from five o'clock until seven every evening of spring break. What if Mike had blabbed my secret to his mom, the nurse? Our mothers would run into each other in the corridor. Mom would recognize Mrs. Humphrey's wide mouth and say, "Didn't we meet on the Y mother-daughter camping trip last month? I'm Sandy Burk."

"Hmm." Mrs. Humphrey would think. "Burk. Oh, yes! Mitzi's mother. Gosh, my son told me all about your horrible disease—I had no idea that you were so sick when I met you! Are you here at the hospital for treatments?"

By the time Mom left to go to the hospital each evening, I'd be almost done shaking from the night before. Mom came home telling us that the group leader passed out slices of diseased human lungs in baggies for them to examine. Mom and the other cigarette addicts called each other between meetings to trade pep talks.

"Haven't seen any rats, yet," Mom whispered to me after the third night. "But I'm on the lookout!" Apparently she hadn't seen Mike's mother either, thank goodness.

I almost told Birdy the whole story about sixty-five times, but I didn't. Maybe when we were old—REALLY old—I would tell her. For the time being, however, I decided it was better to map out a plan for ending the whole thing. But how? Could I tell Mike my mom was dead? I pictured myself at the funeral, dressed in black. I'm a tragic figure, tear-streaked but beautiful. There are other mourners wailing and shrieking, but not I. I carry my sorrow in silence with grace and dignity.

My entire school is there to pay their respects. They weep at the sight of me, their hearts breaking. But my eyes are lowered and I do not look at any of them.

Finally, one heart-wrenching sob escapes my lips. I look like I'm about to faint! Mike Humphrey pushes the other kids aside and rushes to catch me before I fall. He holds me in his strong arms, but I am too grief-stricken to notice the look of pure love radiating from his handsome face.

YECCH! I couldn't have Mom die, even if it was just pretend. And besides, I'd have a lot of explaining to do if Mrs. Humphrey and my "dead" mother ran into each other at the hospital.

So, I decided to have Mom miraculously cured instead. Here's how it would go: The doctors have given up. Even my father has lost hope. But not me. I've sent everyone away, and without a thought for my own comfort, I selflessly tend to Mom's every need, gently spooning soup through her chapped lips and whispering words of encouragement.

They try to pull me away, fearing that I, too, will sicken. But I refuse to budge. And at last, against all odds and medical predictions, Mom recovers!

The doctors are in awe. Specialists gather from around the world to study her X rays. "It's amazing!" the experts say.

"You're an inspiration to us all," the surgeon general tells me at the press conference. Reporters cheer, cameras flash. Newspaper headlines read, "Daughter's Love Saves Mom!" I appear on all of the TV talk shows. Everyone watches, especially Mike Humphrey.

I was at Birdy's house the last day of vacation when Roxy called to say she was back in town. Birdy was so excited it made me gag.

"Me? I'm not doing anything," Birdy said into the phone. "Wanna come over? Great!" She hung up and looked at me. "Oh," she said. Like, "Oh, YOU'RE here."

"You're not doing ANYTHING? I'm NOTH-ING?" I asked, trying not to cry.

"I didn't mean it that way," Birdy said.

"But I'm dismissed, right?" I said. "Excused? Free to go?"

"Don't be snotty," Birdy said. Then, softening a teeny bit, she said, "Sorry, Mitzi, but you understand, don't you?"

"Not really," I admitted.

Birdy shrugged her shoulders and looked helpless, as if all of this was out of her control.

When I got home, Mom gave me the same helpless shrug. I guess the cigarette burning between her fingers wasn't her fault, either.

"What about your group-quit?" I asked. "Your hospital friends? Your meetings?"

"Last night was the last meeting. It was only a one-week program," she sighed. "And anyway, how could I possibly go back to work and face Jake on a fresh quit?"

I shrugged back at her. I could shrug shoulders with the best of them.

★ ★ ★

Birdy's mom called me later to ask if I knew where Birdy was.

I didn't know, and I said so.

"Do you know Roxy's phone number?" she asked.

"No," I said. "We're not friends."

"Do you know her last name?"

"Gold-something," I said. "Goldrush? Goldmine?"

"Well, did Birdy tell you she was going anywhere today?" Miriam asked.

"No," I confessed, suddenly embarrassed not to know. Miriam didn't notice. She just said, "OK, thanks," and hung up.

Birdy called that night and said, "What did you tell my mother?"

"Tell her about what?" I asked.

"About Nathan. Did you tell her anything about Nathan?"

"How come he's Nathan and not Nate-the-Skate or Jazzman or something?" I asked Birdy—or rather, Bobby.

"Did you tell her about him or not?" Birdy asked again, her voice pretty hard, considering it was a whisper.

"Not."

"You sure?"

"I'm sure," I said. "So, where were you?"

"I wasn't anywhere," she said.

"Oh, I've been there," I said as a little joke. Birdy did not laugh.

"You're sure you didn't tell my mom anything about him?"

"You're being really boring, BOBBY," I said and hung up.

Vacation was over. Birdy and I were "polite" to each other at the bus stop the next morning.

"How are you?"

"Fine. How are you?"

"Fine." That was our long-standing code meaning, "I think you're a turd on toast." "Ditto and double for me."

# 9
# A Breakup
# and a Confession

Forget Birdy. I had more important things on my mind. I had to cure my mom. I started looking for Mike the second I got off the bus. I didn't see him, but I saw Vanessa. She saw me, too, and was coming right toward me. Probably to warn me to keep my grubby mitts off her boyfriend. I braced myself.

Then Vanessa touched my arm and said, "Mitzi, I heard about your mother. My dad had cancer, so I know what you're going through. If you ever want to talk . . ."

"WHAT?" I yelped. "Mike TOLD you? It was supposed to be a secret!"

"Illness is nothing to be ashamed of," Vanessa

said. "And Michael thought I might be able to help."

I thought I was going to faint.

"Some of the medications they give your mother might make her seem sicker than the disease actually does," Vanessa said.

I was frozen like a deer caught in the headlights of a car. Not that I've ever actually *seen* a deer caught in the headlights of a car, but still, I was stuck to the spot, eyes and mouth wide open, unable to swallow, blink, or duck.

"My father's hair all fell out," Vanessa explained. "And he got very weak and nauseated."

That thawed me. "I DON'T WANT TO TALK ABOUT IT!" I screamed and ran to the bathroom.

I stood panting in the toilet stall, knowing that I had to cure my mother *immediately*. This had to end. I pictured Mike and Vanessa together, talking about me and my mother. The image of it made me sick, sick, sick.

I had to tell Mike about my mom's miraculous recovery, quick! I also had to tell him to keep his big mouth shut. I did NOT appreciate him leaking my secrets to that Vanessa person.

"If it's a girlfriend you want," I'd tell Mike, "you don't have to settle for a major creep like her. You could just ask ME right now to be your girlfriend, and I'd say YES!"

"YOU? You'd let ME be your boyfriend?" Mike would gasp. "I never dreamed that such a thing was possible!" Then he'd do cartwheels and handstands to celebrate his fabulous luck.

But when I got to class, Mike wasn't there.

I sat next to Fern on the bus ride home and asked her if she wanted to come over. I had to have someone to walk home with, ignoring Birdy. But Fern pointed to her uniform, meaning that she had Girl Scouts. "I can't," she said, "but how about tomorrow? Or are you WORKING tomorrow?"

I didn't need her tomorrow. I needed her right then. So I said I wasn't sure if I'd have to work the next day.

"Well, I have to know so I can tell my mom," Fern said.

"Tell her you might have to go home with me and you might not," I said.

I got off the bus and kept a proper distance behind Roxy Gold-turd and my ex-friend Bobby. Suddenly Roxy spun around and bared her teeth at me. For a second I thought she was going to bite me, but then I realized it was a smile.

"Hi, Mitzi! Your last name is Burk, right?" she asked me.

I nodded.

"Are you by any chance Les Burk's sister?"

"Yeah," I admitted, as she fell in step beside me. Birdy looked as puzzled as I felt.

"He's on the ninth-grade basketball team with my sister's boyfriend's cousin Jason," Roxy chirped. "He's such a doll!"

"Jason?" I asked, confused.

Roxy said, "No, not Jason. Your brother!"

"A doll?" I asked. "Les? Les Burk?"

Roxy laughed. "Oh, you're just as funny as he is! It must be really fun at your house. I bet he's a great big brother." Then she said, "Wow, is THIS where he lives?" as if our house were a national monument. "Bobby, I can't believe you never told me you lived practically NEXT DOOR to Les Burk!"

Birdy looked blankly at my house as if she had never seen it before. It dawned on me that Roxy was dying to come inside and sniff around, but I didn't invite her in.

"Well, bye," I said.

"Do you think your brother's home right now?" Roxy called after me.

I knew Les was at his clarinet lesson, but I said, "I don't know" and closed the door. I'd have given anything to read Birdy's mind right then. She hated Les as much as I did.

Even though we weren't speaking to each other, I couldn't resist calling Birdy as soon as I was sure Roxy was gone.

"I thought she liked Todd Ullah," I teased.

"She broke up with him. And Nathan just called—I guess we broke up, too."

"Oh," I said. "Are you heartbroken?"

Birdy said, "No." But you're not best friends with someone your whole life without learning a thing or two. I knew Birdy was about three and a half seconds away from tears. That took all the fun out of teasing her about Roxy and my brother.

"Going to Birdy's," I called to Mom, who was collapsed on the couch again, suffering from Jake burnout.

"Umph," she replied.

By the time I charged into her room, Birdy was crying. "Nathan broke up with me to be loyal to Todd. Wasn't that nice?"

"Nice?" I asked.

"Well, it was nice of him to stick by his friend like that," sniffed Birdy.

I didn't think that this was a very good time to mention Birdy's disloyalty to me. Instead, I said, "So you think it was nice of Nathan to break up with you?"

Birdy looked at me for a second, then smiled a

little. "That doesn't sound right, does it?" she said and blew her nose with a honk.

The next morning I explained to Fern that I had to take my dog to the vet after school. "He won't get in the car with anyone but me," I said. "And he's really sick." I wanted to tell her that I'd gotten my friend back so I didn't need another one right now, except in emergencies, but I stuck to the dog story instead.

Roxy bounced up to me in the hall before class. "Hi, Mitzi!" she chirped breathlessly.

"Hi."

"So, tell your brother, Les, 'hi!' for me, OK?"

I said, "If you insist."

Roxy smiled, showing me every single tooth she owned, as if it were a dental exam. Then she scampered away.

Mike was absent AGAIN. Why? Where was he? Had he been kidnapped and nobody realized it yet? Was he sick and calling out my name in his feverish delirium? Worse, what if he'd moved away? I bet Vanessa knew where he was, but I'd rather scrub toilets than ask her anything. Whenever I accidentally looked in her direction, she gave me drippy smiles, meant to fill me with courage, I supposed.

Or to welcome me into the girls-with-sick-parents club. How could Mike fall for such a sap?

When I got on the bus to go home, Roxy scooted over and patted the seat next to her, mashing Birdy up against the window. I said, "No, that's OK," and I went and sat with Fern.

"I hope your dog is all right," Fern said.

"Dog?" Then I remembered. "Thanks," I mumbled and changed the subject. "So, Fern, you know that friend of yours who's Mike Humphrey's sister?"

Fern nodded.

"Did she move away or anything?" I asked.

Fern shook her head no and said, "Why?"

I couldn't think of a "why" fast enough, so I just shrugged and looked out the window until my stop. Birdy and I got off. As we choked on the bus's parting fumes, I told her that Roxy wanted me to tell my brother she said "hi."

Birdy asked if I was going to.

"Sure," I smirked.

And I did tell him. After all, I'd said I would.

"LE-ESSS, Roxy Gold-whatever said to tell you she says HI-III!"

"Are you speaking to me, Twerp?" was his reply. "Did I say you could speak to me?"

"She thinks you are SOOOO funny!" I said,

dodging out of his way. "She thinks it must be SOOOO much fun having you as a brother!" I ducked as he lunged at me, and I streaked away. If Les ever had a speck of interest in Roxy Gold-mud, it was squelched forever now. Hee, hee, hee.

"I told him," I said to Birdy on the phone. "You can tell your pal that the message has been sent."

"What did he say?" Birdy asked.

"He said he has always admired Roxy's mind." I giggled. "And that he thinks she's a really interesting person."

I thought Birdy would know I was kidding, but she said, "Wow."

Mike finally showed up at school the next day. He'd had the flu. Plain old flu.

The first chance that I got, I told him that my mom was having surgery and that the doctors felt really great about it. They were sure they could fix her and she'd be perfectly fine.

"So when's the operation?" he asked, except it sounded like "oberation" because his nose was still all stuffed up.

"Tomorrow," I said. "No, I mean—next week, Wednesday. Tomorrow they start doing some stuff, but they don't, um, actually cut her open until next Tuesday—I mean Wednesday."

"Good luck," he said, smiling a bit of his ultra-smile at me.

"Thanks," I said, but in my head I was screaming, "I DON'T EVEN KNOW IF MY MOM'S OPERATION IS TOMORROW OR NEXT WEDNESDAY??"

Birdy wasn't on the bus home, but Fern invited herself over. She'd told her mom that if she didn't come home it was because she was at my house and she'd call as soon as she walked in my door.

"Oh, all right," I said.

Fern thought that we should do homework first. When I suggested we were shipwrecked on a desert island and we were doing these math problems to keep our minds sharp while we waited to be rescued, Fern looked at me like I was totally bonkers and said, "Shipwrecked?"

"OK so we're prisoners," I suggested, "and we're being forced to do this homework under penalty of death."

"Huh?" Fern said.

"If we don't finish it in time, we'll be tortured. Probably in really slow, horrible ways," I explained.

"That's stupid," Fern said.

It turned out that she didn't want to pretend we were anything! She just wanted to do homework.

Then, right in front of my dad, Fern asked where my dog was. I had to shove her out of the room and tell her that the dog had died and that talking about it around my grief-stricken father was mean. At least Fern had the sense to be ashamed. And at least my mom came home all tattered and Jake-weary and headed straight for the couch, looking like a proper invalid. That would come in handy in case Fern happened to see Mike's sister again.

It took forever for Fern's dad to come pick her up.

After dinner, Birdy called and told me to come over. I flew out the door. I couldn't wait to tell her that Fern had been over and we'd had a total blast (a mini stretcher). The pastor was standing on the church steps, so I had to veer from my usual path and wave innocently to him from the sidewalk.

Miriam stopped me the minute I got to the door and said, "Roberta's grounded, Mitzi. She can't play with you."

"Grounded?" I'd never heard of Birdy being grounded before. And I'd never heard Miriam call her Roberta either!

Miriam looked miserable. "Well, I guess it's OK if *you* go on up, just for just a bit." She sighed.

I ran up to Birdy's room.

"Your mom says you're grounded!" I said. "What did you do?"

"Roxy's dad caught us smoking behind the garage." Birdy shrugged as if it was no big deal.

"SMOKING?" I gasped. "As in CIGARETTES?"

Birdy wasn't looking at me.

"For real? You SMOKED?"

She still wasn't looking at me.

"Why?" I asked.

Birdy ignored my question and said, "I can't go anywhere after school or see Roxy for a week."

"So how come your mom is letting me see you?" I asked.

Birdy shrugged. "Maybe she thinks you'll lecture me because of your mom or something."

I was tempted to do just that. But I had been on the receiving end of enough lectures to know better. I was completely floored that Birdy had smoked, but I tried to sound normal. "Well, how'd you like it?" I asked.

"Smoking?"

"Yeah."

Birdy shrugged. "It was OK." Then she shook her head. "Actually, it was puke-city. It tasted gross and made me dizzy. It burned my throat and made my tongue feel hairy. I coughed my brains out. And afterward I had a killer headache."

"But besides that it was pretty good?" I asked.

Birdy smiled at me, but it was a sheepish smile.

Not that I've ever seen a sheep smile, but there it was—a soggy, sorry, shamefaced smile. Her freckles started to brighten like stars coming out at night. "I don't blame you if you think I'm a stupid idiot for smoking," Birdy said.

That was my cue.

"Talk about stupid," I said. "Wait till you hear what I did." And out gushed the whole Stripitis story.

When I was done, Birdy stared at me with her mouth flapping open.

"I did it for love," I explained, hoping that made it sound more heroic than pathetic.

Birdy's mouth shut, but her eyes stayed huge. I couldn't tell what she was thinking. "Aren't you going to say anything?" I asked.

"STRIPITIS? Mitzi! What if Vanessa or Mike Humbug or someone or EVERYONE finds out it's not true?"

"His name is HUMPHREY!" I said for the ninety-eighth time.

Birdy started to laugh. Eyebrows first, then eyes, and a sniff through her nose. Then she opened her mouth and hooted. Pretty soon her whole body was shaking with laughter. I'd swear it was even coming out her ears.

And I laughed, too, with great yucks and snorts of relief. It felt good, good, good not to be alone with the lie anymore. And Birdy didn't think it was crazy. She thought it was hilarious!

Best of all, I'd cheered her up and made her forget all about her lame crime with Roxy Gold-rot. After all, any jerk can smoke. You only had to be STUPID to smoke. Well, maybe you had to be stupid to do what I'd done, too—but my crime took more than stupidity. It took creativity and guts!

# 10
## The Bellyache and the Envelope

During Birdy's grounded week, she kept sitting with Roxy on the bus. But another girl from their class, Talia, sat with them too. I noticed that Birdy looked a little blotchy when Roxy got off the bus with Talia. I knew *that* feeling, but I was far too kind to gloat about it.

By the following Tuesday, I had all the details worked out about my mother's surgery. I was calm, cool, and in control. If only I had a trench coat and could raise one eyebrow at a time, I'd have made a perfect spy.

I told Mike that Mom's operation was scheduled for early the next morning.

"I'll have my mom check on things for you, if you want," he offered.

I'd planned for that. "Thanks," I said calmly. "But she's not at your mom's hospital anymore. She's at Mt. Sinai now." PLEASE, I thought desperately, don't tell me your dad works there! He didn't.

For the rest of the day I acted like a girl whose mother was going to be operated on in the morning. Scared but hopeful. It was a great relief to have this whole thing almost over with. In a few days I could tell Mike that my mom was fine. He'd say, "That's nice," and that would be that.

Roxy left Talia on the bus that afternoon and got off with Birdy again. I was so busy thinking about Mom's operation the next morning that it took me a second to realize Roxy was at my side.

When we reached my house, she said she was really, really thirsty and asked if she could come in for a glass of water. Birdy did not mention that her house had running water too.

I knew Les was at band practice, but I didn't say anything. I let them in. Roxy looked all around at the Burk family museum. She practically wept over Les's baby picture on the wall. I'd never seen anyone drink a glass of water that slowly, especially someone who was really, really thirsty.

Then Roxy said she was dying to see my bedroom. I led her upstairs, with Birdy trudging along behind. Roxy glanced quickly into my room. Then she turned to the real point of her visit. "Is this Les's room?" she asked, her eyes all twinkly as she tried his doorknob.

"It's always locked," I said. "But for ten bucks I'll break in."

Birdy glared at me. Roxy's toothy smile faded a notch. I don't know if she was considering my price or if she realized that she was acting like a twit.

Finally I said, "Oh, in case you were hoping to run into my brother, he's at marching band until six o'clock."

Roxy instantly plunked down her glass of water, snatched up her backpack, and headed for the front door. It was *my* turn to smile.

"Have you known Les long?" Roxy asked Birdy on their way out.

"All my life," Birdy muttered. She didn't add that he'd never once been civil to her or that she'd despised him since birth.

After Birdy and Roxy left, I stuffed my face and then hid some more food in my room for later. I wouldn't be eating in front of anyone for a while because my plan was to fake a stomach bug. After all, I couldn't very well show up at school on the day of Mom's operation! I had to pace the hospital corridors and give moral support to my terrified father and brother. Someone had to hold my family together in this time of crisis.

I parked myself in Mom's spot on the couch. When she came home from teaching she found me there, moaning softly and wearing my droopy-eyed stomachache face. It took all my strength to explain that the mystery meat at lunch had tasted fishy.

It was my most brilliant acting job ever, and I was allowed to stay home from school the next day. Dad stayed with me. We played so many games of Scrabble that the tiles began to dance in front of my eyes and I started feeling sick for real.

Then Birdy called. "How was the operation?" she giggled.

"It was touch and go for a while," I said. "But the doctors pulled her through. It looks like she's going to live!"

Birdy laughed like a lunatic.

When Dad went to his music room to practice, I dashed into the kitchen and gobbled up everything in sight. I hadn't had a single crumb to eat since devouring my secret stash the night before, and I still had a long way to go because I hoped to squeeze one more day out of my stomach drama.

It worked so well that before noon the next day, Dad said he thought he'd better take me to the doctor. So I perked up and had a little snack.

"What was it, a math test?" he asked.

"What do you mean?" I asked back.

"A paper due that you hadn't written?"

"I have no idea what you're talking about!" I huffed. Then I got dressed and Dad drove me to school.

I walked into class, and everybody got quiet. Ms. London came up and put her arm around me. "Mitzi dear, how's your mother doing?" she asked in a quiet voice.

If I'd ever blushed before, it was nothing compared to that moment. I'm sure I was blood-red from scalp to toenail, and I felt sweat drops leaping off of me the way they do in cartoons. Ms. London handed me a big white envelope and said, "We were going to mail these to you. We didn't expect you to be back so soon."

I felt my entire body shrink to one humiliated speck. Unfortunately, I didn't disappear completely. I looked down at the envelope in my hand. On the front it said, in loopy script, *Dear Mitzi, Our hearts are with you!* And then it was signed by everyone in the whole class.

I could guess what was inside: get-well cards for my mom. I glanced at Vanessa, and she smiled her sticky smile. This was her idea. Look at her, so proud of herself for blowing my secret. She was despicable, mucking around in other people's lives.

I sat down with my envelope and continued to sweat. I didn't look at anyone. I just stared at the top of my desk. They'd think I was overwhelmed with gratitude. So touched by their kindness that I was knocked speechless. Or maybe I was so worried about my mom that I couldn't lift my head.

Everyone knew. Everyone.

I supposed I could say that Mike must have misunderstood something I'd said. Or I could say that Vanessa made it all up just to make me look stupid. Why? Because she was jealous. She knew Mike really liked me and was only pretending to like her because I wouldn't have anything to do with him.

But it was too late for any of that. I'd missed my chance. The second Ms. London handed me that envelope, I should have said, "What are you talking about? I was just out with a bellyache!" Ha! That would have made Vanessa look pretty stupid. Then again, it would also have made Mike Humphrey hate me forever and curse me till the grave.

I snuck a quick peek at him. His head hung low, probably with pity for me. Or maybe with shame for blabbing my secret. No, wait, he was looking down at something—reading something. It was a COMIC BOOK! He wasn't even thinking about me! He was reading one of those incredibly stupid superhero comic books like Les used to read. YEESH! I couldn't believe it. He was just another numb-headed, dorky boy like my brother.

*Poof!* My crush was gone. I felt my forehead and took my pulse—no Mike Humphrey fever or racing heart. I imagined him standing really close to me, smiling his full ultra-grin, and I felt NOTHING. It was finished.

How amazing, I thought. One minute a person— me in particular—would do or say anything to get a boy's attention, and then a minute later that boy is just . . . just . . . a plain old, nothing-special, superhero-comic-book-reading boy! Well, maybe if he'd liked me back at least a little, it would have made a difference. But he had probably never even been interested in my mom's disease at all. He had just pretended he was to impress Vanessa.

I went back to staring at my desktop, and that hot blush started spreading again like flames across every bit of me. Could people actually burn to a cinder from embarrassment? I pictured a little pile of ashes on the seat of my desk—Mitzi Burk, incinerated by shame.

After class, Vanessa said she was sorry if she'd embarrassed me, but she didn't think I should be alone at a time like this. She wanted me to know that everyone cared about me. I bet she expected me to THANK her! But not a peep came out of my mouth. What could I peep?

Luckily, there's nothing particularly strange about a girl not speaking to or looking at anyone the day after her mother has had an operation.

The rest of the day was entirely unbearable, and the hands of the clock slogged around as if they were clogged with mud. But finally it was time to leave. I got on the bus and sat by the window. I didn't even look up to see where Birdy sat.

Fern plopped down next to me and said, "Gee, first your dog died and now your mother's sick!"

"Meaning *what?*" I barked, like my imaginary dog.

"Meaning you have lousy luck," Fern said.

As if that wasn't bad enough, Roxy came to the back of the bus to say, "I just can't believe it about your mom."

Panic. She couldn't believe it as in "Wow, that's amazing," or she couldn't believe it as in "You must be lying"? I held my breath.

"I was just at your house the other day, and you didn't say a word!" Roxy said.

"THUMP, THUMP!" That was my heart.

"You are such a brave girl."

I exhaled.

"Tell your brother I'll pray for him. For your mother, too, of course. OK?" Roxy went back to sit with Talia, and I went back to staring out the window.

When I got off the bus, Birdy was right behind me. I asked her if she'd heard.

"It's not such a big school," Birdy said. "I'm sure *everyone* has heard."

"I have to move," I moaned. "And not just to another school. To a whole different state. How do I make my parents move?"

We stopped and sat on the steps of the church.

"Well, you could try burning down your house," Birdy said.

"Nah," I said. "What else?"

"How about if you fill the house with snakes?"

"Come on, Birdy," I said. "Where would I get SNAKES?"

"If you don't like my ideas," Birdy pouted, "solve your own problems."

"No, no," I said. "Fire, snakes—they're both really good ideas. But keep thinking. I have to come up with something fast! I can't EVER go back to that school."

"Then how are you going to see your beloved Mike Humphrey?"

"His name's not—wait. Did you say *Humphrey*?"

Birdy nodded.

"I don't like him anymore," I said. "I don't know why I ever did. He's a nobody. I think I completely made him up in my head!"

Birdy's laugh bubbled up beside me, and in spite of how totally miserable I was, it made me giggle too. Not a happy giggle, though. It was a sort of insane giggle that turned into hiccups.

"Maybe you'd better run away," Birdy offered after our hysterics calmed.

I saw myself on the road, the wind in my hair. Fearless. Tough, but with a heart of gold. Farmers let me sleep in their haystacks, and I slopped their hogs in return.

"Mitzi," Birdy said, interrupting my thoughts. "You could try telling the truth."

"The WHAT?" That was me, horrified. "To the whole school? On the P.A. system? 'Attention, all classes. My mother is not, and never has been, sick. I was just kidding, hee hee'? Come on, Birdy, get serious!"

"Well, then, what about doing nothing?" she suggested. "Zip, zilch, nada?"

## Flake Off and Spill

I took Birdy's advice and did absolutely nothing. When people asked how my mother was, I said, "Fine," which was the truth.

Thanks to Fern, everyone in After-School had heard about the operation. At first all their attention felt good and I was tempted, for a split second, to describe the gruesome symptoms of Stripitis. But then I remembered the envelope of get-well cards, and the temptation evaporated.

Now that Roxy had Talia, she had no more use for Birdy. Thank goodness, because my problems were so gigantic I really needed Birdy all to myself.

"Life is a minefield," I told her one evening on the church steps. "The After-School counselor said she wanted to bring over a casserole!"

"That was nice of her," Birdy said. "How'd you stop her?"

"I told the truth. I said my entire family, every last one of us, despises casseroles."

"Some people don't ask before they come over," Birdy said. "When my uncle Joe died, people just showed up and brought Aunt Frieda food by the truckload."

"Well, no one died here," I said. But then I was scared. What if people DID start showing up with casseroles?

"Maybe you could pretend to be my mom," I said. "We'd put makeup on you to make you look pale and sickly, maybe put a scarf or something on your head, and stick you in her bed. You'd just have to cough and moan a lot. No one would get too close."

Birdy giggled.

"Is that a 'yes' giggle or a 'no' giggle?" I asked.

"Where would your real mom be while I was moaning in her bed? Locked in the closet?" Birdy giggled some more. I guessed it was a 'no' giggle.

Then another scary thought occurred to me. "Birdy?" I panicked. "Do you think my mom has to write a thank-you letter to everyone in my class for their get-well cards?"

"I suppose so," Birdy groaned in sympathy. "But she's probably not up to it—yet."

"That's true," I agreed. "She's still way too tired and full of stitches."

"Maybe in a few weeks, though, you can add forging your mother's signature to your list of crimes," Birdy said.

Dad was working on his program notes at the kitchen table when I got home from school. "Ever hear of Niccolo Paganini?" he asked me.

"No."

"Greatest violinist who ever lived. He composed such intricate and tricky violin music that people accused him of being a witch."

"Is he playing at your concert?" I asked.

"He can't. He died in 1840."

I shifted from foot to foot, wondering why Dad was telling me this.

"All that talent," Dad said, "but no respect for the law. They say he spent more time in jail than out of it."

Did Dad give me a meaningful look when he said that?

"Boom, boom, boom," said my heart.

Later Birdy called to tell me that Roxy and Talia saw my brother at the mall. The way Birdy pronounced "Taaaliaa" was pure sneer, but that wasn't the point. The point was that Roxy had gone up to Les and said, "I'm glad your mom is going to be OK." And apparently Les had then told her to "flake off."

For once my brother did something to make me proud! But I had to cross my fingers and hope he wouldn't get asked any more questions about Mom. If he found out what I'd done, he'd tell my parents in a heartbeat. The thought made me shudder.

On the bus ride home the next day, Birdy was sitting with Roxy again. I had one teeny pang of jealousy, but it went away when I saw the expression on Birdy's face. It was definitely not a look of happiness. And as soon as we got off the bus, I knew it wasn't joy dripping down her cheeks either.

"Nathan likes Roxy," she sniffled.

"Your old Nathan? The Taft Nathan?" I asked.

Birdy nodded. "He asked her to be his girlfriend."

"The creep," I said sympathetically.

"Roxy told him she had to ask me if I minded! I'm totally embarrassed," Birdy whispered. "Totally. Roxy thinks it was sweet of him to wait a decent length of time after we broke up before asking her."

"Mr. Sweet and Decent," I said.

"And I can tell she thinks it's really nice of them both to be so concerned with my feelings."

"Well, two really nice people," I said, "deserve each other."

"Know what the worst part is?" she asked. "That Nathan pretended to like me just so he could be near Roxy!" Birdy shivered with embarrassment.

"Do you still love him?" I asked.

"Eeeew, no!" Birdy said, "I never really liked him all that much. I only went out with him because Roxy was with Todd."

"Let me get this straight," I said. "You went out with Nathan because Roxy was with Todd. And Nathan went out with you because Roxy was with Todd?"

Birdy and I furrowed our brows at each other. Then we started laughing so hard that I thought we'd choke.

That Saturday, Mom told me to get ready for my dad's concert.

"What concert?" I asked, instantly panicking. I had no idea how long it took someone to recover from surgery, but I was pretty sure this was too soon for Mom to be seen out in public. She looked lousy from Jake-sickness, but not *that* lousy.

"I think it's Paganini," Mom said.

"I HATE PAGANINI," I said.

Mom looked at me funny. "I thought you and Daddy and I could grab some lunch beforehand. Maybe poke around in a few art galleries?"

"What about Les?"

"He's not coming."

"No fair! How come he gets to stay home?"

Mom squinted at me. "He has too much home-work to do."

"Me too!" I said. "I'll stay home with him."

That cracked her up. "It would be on the eleven o'clock news. 'Brother and sister torment each other to death in suburbia.'" Mom laughed. "Get in the shower. Get dressed."

When we got to the auditorium, I rushed Mom to our seats and scrunched down, pulling my hair over my face and hating the fact that we had aisle seats. But, of course, because that's just EXACTLY the way life is, Mike Humphrey was instantly standing in the aisle next to us with Vanessa and an old guy.

"Hello, Mitzi," Vanessa said. "This is my dad."

I grunted. Then there was a hairy pause. Mom shot me a where-are-your-manners look, which I pretended not to see. Then she smiled up at the three intruders. "How do you do," she said, sticking out her hand. "I'm Mitzi's mom, Sandy Burk."

"Mrs. Burk!" Vanessa gasped. "You look fantastic! That's amazing. What's it been, a week or two?"

I could not possibly have sunk any lower in my seat without lying flat on the floor.

Vanessa turned to her father. "This is the lady I was telling you about."

The man smiled at Mom. "Vanessa wants me to tell you about the support group I'm in. I've found it very helpful. Newcomers are always welcome."

"You're a smoker?" my mom asked, thinking it was that kind of support group.

"Nope, never was," he said. "But we better find our seats. We'll talk more at intermission." And they scurried off, the damage done.

Mom's expression went from confused to suspicious. I grabbed the program notes and pretended to be searching busily for Dad's name. Finally the lights went down. When the music started, I snuck a peek at Mom's face. Uh-oh.

I didn't hear one single note of that symphony.

When the lights came on for intermission, Mom looked me in the eye and said, "Would you like to tell me what that was about, or should we go find your friends in the lobby?" I didn't like either one of those options, so I didn't pick one.

Mom said, "Let's go for a walk."

We scooted down the row and out the side exit. I waited while she tried to light a cigarette against the wind. Then she faced me and said, "Spill."

What choice did I have? Well, I thought up a few quick choices, but they all involved pretty big stretchers. No, they were actual lies, and I was sick to death of lying. So I spilled.

Mom was silent at first, listening to my story, but then she started to mumble things under her breath. When I got to the part about calling the disease *Stripitis*, Mom's muttering became sputtering. She smoked one cigarette after another, lighting each one off the last one, not even bothering with matches. I didn't actually SEE steam coming out of her ears, but I could feel the anger sizzling off her as I pushed on with my story.

When I got to the operation part, Mom froze to the spot and said in a very quiet, very steady voice, "Could you repeat that?"

I cleared my throat, but my voice still squeaked. "I said your operation was successful and your life was saved."

That's when Mom lost it.

I had heard the expression "hopping mad" before, but I'd never seen it in action until Mom was actually jumping furiously right there on the sidewalk.

"How COULD you?" *(Hop, hop.)* "How could you concoct such a scenario at my expense?" *(Hop.)* "What kind of daughter could even THINK, let alone SAY, something like that about her own MOTHER?" (One more *hop*.)

Then, *thud*. Done hopping. Mom suddenly seemed to weigh several tons. "Go on," she said, in a tired, five-hundred-year-old voice.

So I did, although I would much rather have been struck by lightning. I told her about Vanessa telling my teacher and my whole class. Then I explained that Vanessa was the girl Mom had just met, with her dad, and that the boy with them was Mike Humphrey—the guy it all started with—the guy I didn't like anymore. And then I had nothing else to say.

We stood in total silence for a second with Mom not looking at me. Then she stiffly checked her watch and turned, crisp as a soldier, to march back inside. I scurried after her. At the door she said, "We'll discuss this with your father, of course."

Dread.

Dread, dread, dread, dread, dread.

There was Dad, all chipper and smiles, waiting for us in the greenroom. Why did he always have to be so happy after a concert? Mom kept quiet until we got into the car. Then she told him, through clenched teeth, that we had a family problem and had to have a talk.

Dad glanced at my mom and then back at me. "Maybe we should stop for ice cream," he said.

"This is beyond ice cream," Mom said.

That stunned him. I don't think we'd ever had a problem that outdistanced ice cream before. Dad drove us home in dazed silence. Neither Mom nor I spoke.

We sat at the kitchen table, and I had to tell the whole story all over again. Dad looked at me as if he had never seen me before. Mom stared at her hands. When I got to the part about the envelope of get-well cards, Dad exhaled all the air he had ever breathed, and Mom put her head down on the table. She made sniffly noises that sounded a lot like crying.

When I was done, the room, the house, our yard, block, subdivision, county, and state became nothing but an enormous silence that a person could easily drown in.

After a lifetime of that, Mom looked up and said, "I take some responsibility for this."

"Why on earth would YOU feel responsible?" Dad asked.

"Well, for lots of reasons," Mom said. "Because I smoke, and I never realized how upsetting that is for Mitzi. And because I've been so preoccupied lately with teaching that I haven't been paying her the attention she deserves and obviously needs."

"Whoa," Dad said. "This is about a huge, snowballing lie that Mitzi told, all by herself. I don't want you to bail her out like that."

Just then, Les loped into the room. I had completely forgotten he was even home. I sure didn't want him in on this discussion. I was already feeling humiliated enough. "I bet this meeting is about Ma's operation," he said casually, taking a bite of an apple. "Am I right?"

My hair stood on end. "How did YOU know?"

He didn't say who told him. He just smirked and said, "It's such a typical fungus-brained kind of lie. Not that anyone's shocked. Am I right?" He looked from Mom to Dad. "Is anyone here surprised?"

Well, of course they're surprised! I thought. Why wouldn't they be? But when I looked at my parents, they weren't saying anything.

"You do have a little problem with the truth," Mom said.

"*Little?*" Les scoffed.

"WHAT?" That was me, offended. "A slightly overactive imagination, maybe, but—"

"Plague-carrying rats at Seventh-Day Adventist? A rule against After-School mothers socializing with each other?" Mom reminded me.

"Our DOG died?!" Dad added. "Mitzi, there's a difference between having an overactive imagination and telling lies."

"But they weren't really SEPARATE lies. They were just part of one BIG lie," I offered hopefully.

Mom sighed. "I think that's enough for one day," she said. "We'll talk more tomorrow."

Slow torture. I pictured my family gathering around the table night after night to discuss my lie. This would go down in family history as "The Year of the Lie." Everything would be dated by it. "Did we get the blue car before The Year of the Lie or after?" "Remember that big flood? It was AFTER The Year of the Lie, wasn't it?"

# 12
## The Plan and the Countdown

"Sounds totally awful!" Birdy said the next day.

"And I have to suffer through more awfulness tonight. I swear, I'm going to be Honest Abe from now on." I sighed.

"Yeah, right," Birdy said.

"What's that supposed to mean?" I said. "It's not like I'm such a big liar. I told one lie, period."

"Your nose is growing," Birdy said.

I was trying to decide whether to be offended or to laugh, when I realized I didn't have the strength for either.

At our lie conference that evening, my parents announced that they had a plan. I told them that doing nothing seemed to be working OK, but they said, "No."

"We think," Mom said, "that you and I should go together to talk to your class."

"That's a HORRIBLE idea!" I said. "Guaranteed to make every single kid in my class snicker and point at me for the rest of my life!" I could see the principal saying at our graduation ceremony, "And a round of boos, ladies and gentlemen, for the Liar of the Year—Mitzi Burk! Stand up, Mitzi!"

Mom was still talking. "I'll tell your classmates that being the daughter of a smoker put enormous pressure on you, which I believe is true. And you'll tell them you fabricated the whole story and that you're sorry."

"WHAT?" That was me, shrieking.

"You are sorry, aren't you?" Dad asked.

"Of course I am!"

"Sorry that you lied or sorry you got caught?" asked Mom.

I knew that was a trick question. I considered begging and pleading and promising to be perfect for the rest of my life. Actually, I did more than just consider it—I tried it, crying real tears. But it did no good. My parents had their hearts set on propping me up like a bowling pin for my class-mates to knock down.

"Why do you think they call it punishment?" Dad asked.

"Can't you just ground me, like other parents do?" I asked. "Take away my allowance? Say no more desserts for five years or something?"

"We could add those in, if you like," he offered.

"How about if we make a deal, Mom?" I said, stalling for time. "Since you say you feel responsible for causing me all this stress, then here's what would be fair: First, you quit smoking for a whole week. No, two—make that THREE weeks. And after you've done that, gone three weeks without taking a single puff, I'll go to school with you and we'll talk to my class. How's that?"

"Hmmm," Dad said, looking from me to Mom. "Sounds like an interesting bargain to me. Penance and pain all around!"

"You can't be serious," Mom said.

"Why not?" I replied.

"But I'm in the middle of teaching!"

"So?" Dad and I said at the same time.

"One week," Mom offered.

"Three," I demanded, wishing I had suggested three months.

"OK, call it two weeks, and that's final!" Dad declared. "Now shake on it."

So, Mom and I shook hands.

★ ★ ★

I crept to my room and pulled out my calendar. There were exactly twenty-six days until the end of the school year. What were the odds of my mom squeezing a two-week quit into twenty-six days? Twenty-six minus fourteen—she could have up to twelve false starts and still win! I stared at the calendar, each square a day of torment and suspense bringing me one day closer to either victory or humiliation.

I looked out my window at a sparrow perched on the windowsill. He was just standing there, with nothing to fear but cats. I wished I were him.

Mom started trying to quit immediately. She began with a few short quits that each lasted until Jake did his next rotten thing. Lucky for me, he did rotten things daily. But the chunks of time between quits were getting smaller. When one quit failed, Mom would only smoke for half a day, or for one single cigarette, and then she would quickly start the next quit. Those nice long breaks in between to gather strength for the next attempt were a thing of the past. My mother was serious this time— these times.

But it didn't seem to be getting any easier for her. One night she crumpled up a pack at bedtime and then got up in the morning to snatch it out of the trash. I watched her tape together a broken butt and smoke it in the car on her way to the store to buy another pack.

"This is really pathetic," I told my dad, trying to hide my glee.

"If at first you don't succeed, quit, quit again," he said. He looked like a man who'd had all the quitting he could stand.

I dragged myself to school, picturing Mom in front of my class. "Hello, everyone," she'd say. "I want to thank you for your get-well cards, but I never actually received them. My daughter, Mitzi, shoved the whole batch into a neighbor's trash can on her way home from school."

The class gasps.

"Mitzi," Mom continues, "perhaps you'd like to explain your behavior?" She smiles and steps aside.

I cringe, standing there at the front of the room. I'm crying and my nose starts to run. Everyone watches in fascination. Then a tiny voice manages to squeak out of me and say, "My mom wasn't sick. I made it up. Sorry."

There's a moment of silence. Then the first kid stands up and yells something cruel. It's probably Mike Humphrey. Another kid throws a tomato that he'd left in his backpack for six weeks. It hits me, *splat,* in the face. Then everyone starts throwing things—peanut butter and jelly sandwiches, notebooks, stinky gym towels. My mom tries to yell above the noise, "IT'S ALL MY FAULT," but no one hears.

On the fifth day, Mom tried the nicotine patch, but two days later Jake put an end to that quit by hurling jars of paint at the chalkboard. Mom had to move her students into the hall while the custodian cleaned it up. When she told us this story, I tried to look sympathetic. But I was snickering inside. One week down!

My mother puffed out a huge cloud of smoke and hissed, "Jake is not human!" just as Birdy was walking in. I hurried Birdy back outside. I knew she was a Jake sympathizer. Mom would burst into flames if she heard Birdy say Jake just needed love and kindness.

"I see she's smoking," Birdy said. "At this rate, there's no way she'll be able to sacrifice you at the classroom altar."

Birdy and I rode our bikes around and around the church parking lot. "Well," I said, "let's say she does quit smoking for two weeks and I do have to get up in front of my class with her and confess. I was thinking that after she leaves, I could just tell my class that she's nuts!"

"NUTS?" Birdy blurted. "You'd tell them your mother is NUTS?"

"Yeah! I could say that symptom number one of Stripitis is not admitting you have it. What do you think?" I rode closer to Birdy.

"Everyone would look at you fishy-eyed," she giggled. "They'd think Stripitis runs in your family. And if you say you aren't sick, that will prove you ARE sick, because people with Stripitis don't admit they're sick! Right?" This cracked her up.

Nobody asked me about my mother anymore except Fern and Vanessa, which was a relief but also insulting.

"That's how you know who your real friends are," Birdy said. "My mom says most people get bored right away with other people's problems. But your REAL friends keep caring about you no matter what a pain in the butt you've become."

If that was true, then Fern was my best friend on earth. She was sympathy itself. I think Girl Scouts are trained to be sympathetic though.

And Vanessa offered to have her father call my mom about joining his support group. I told her that it would make my mother violently angry.

"Anger is one of the stages of recovery," Vanessa assured me.

The only other person paying me a lot of attention was Mom, which included following me into my bedroom every day to ask me what was new and how school was. Sometimes, when Birdy and I were right in the middle of doing something, Mom would barge in and ask if we wanted to do a jigsaw puzzle or bake cookies with her.

"Don't worry," Birdy said, "she'll get over it. It's like when my mom reads how-to-raise-kids books. They make her act weird for a little while, but then she gets normal again."

In the meantime, Mom bought a juicing machine and spent hours each day, noisily grinding up fruits and vegetables and swilling the juice to drown her addiction.

When Mom explained to Birdy that the poisons from smoking had to be washed out of her system, Birdy smiled politely.

"You know, you girls could probably do with a little detoxing, too, come to think of it. Between the ozone layer depletion, pesticides, preservatives, exhaust fumes, and whatnot, you're both probably full of pollutants." Mom held out a glass of foamy, greenish-gray liquid and said, "Here, Birdy, try this spinach, cabbage, and kale juice."

I could hear alarm bells going off in Birdy's head. I yanked her out of harm's way, meaning out of the kitchen, and called back, "It's OK, Mom, Birdy's already a vegetarian!"

By day number five of the juice-quit, I was a wreck. Then, while I was at After-School, Mom had a meeting with Jake's parents. They told the principal and some big shot from the school board that Jake was a perfect doll at home, and it was all my mother's fault that he acted so disgusting at school. That meeting ended the juice-quit in an exquisite cloud of smoke. PHEW!

Dad was sympathetic at dinner. "We know you would do it all differently if you could, honey," he said, patting my mom's hand. "And I, for one, am impressed by how hard you've been trying to quit." Then he turned to Les and me. "Aren't you proud of Mommy, kids?"

Les grunted his "Yes," and then everyone looked at me.

I didn't know what to say. Proud that she kept failing? Proud that she was so addicted? Scared to death that she'd really quit and send me straight to the electric chair of public humiliation?

"Look at her!" Les snorted, pointing his fork at me. "Mouth gaping open like a carp." I closed my mouth. "She actually believes you're going to rat on her to her class!" He snickered his vile snicker and shook his head.

My parents shot Les a shut-up-or-we'll-kill-you look and then got back to shoveling their dinners into their faces.

Obviously they were as sick of Les's snicker as I was.

The next day Mom was offered a permanent teaching job for September. I guess her principal was so impressed by the fact that she hadn't killed Jake *or* his parents, he figured he could trust Mom with her own class.

"So now I absolutely MUST stop smoking," she informed the family, glaring at us as if the failure of all her earlier quits were our fault. "No more playing around."

There was no cheering. My father and brother barely looked up from their plates.

"Can I go to Birdy's?" I asked.

"This might be it," I told Birdy.

"I'm still betting on you," Birdy assured me. "I don't think your mom can do it. Everyone in the world, practically, has quit smoking except your mother. In fact, if it weren't for her, I bet the tobacco companies would go out of business!"

Hey, was Birdy insulting my mother? No one was allowed to insult my mother except me! I never said bad things about Miriam!

"My mom could quit in a snap," I said, "if she really WANTED to."

Birdy looked up from the lump of clay she was squeezing.

"Never mind," I said with a sigh. "You wanna be cave women? You can be inventing the first pot."

"Sure," Birdy said. She hunched over and started grunting.

## 13
## Tapping and Twins

Exactly fifteen days before the end of the school year, Mom lugged the TV into her room and took to her bed for the weekend. She had rented old black-and-white comedies that the guy at the video store promised were funny.

Dad said it was laugh therapy. "If you've got any funny books or heard any good jokes recently, tell Mommy."

"No way!" I said to myself, eyeing the calendar.

Mom's TV was as loud as Milt's, and she made noises more like strangled hysterics than human laughter. I planned to stay out of my hilarious house as much as possible.

★ ★ ★

"How's the quit going?" Milt asked when I walked into Birdy's kitchen.

"It's a funny one," I said.

Milt nodded as if he knew what I meant. "The tenth time is the charm," he said. "This is about ten, isn't it?"

"At least," I said.

Milt nodded. "Well, it's always good to have a hobby."

"Your dad thinks quitting is my mom's hobby," I told Birdy upstairs.

"Knitting, quitting, whatever!" Birdy giggled, her knitting needles clicking like tiny tap dancers. Then she said, "Roxy called."

"Is she coming over?" I asked. "Should I leave?" My stomach dropped like a rock.

"No, Mitzi." Birdy said, rolling her eyes. "She just called to talk."

The rock lifted a bit. "Talk about what?"

"I'm not sure. I think she's lonely," Birdy said. "I don't think she's best friends with Talia anymore, and Nathan broke up with her."

"Your Nathan? How tragic," I said.

Birdy smiled a nice, mean smile and said, "Roxy only has one girlfriend and one boyfriend at a time.

Like one for each hand. She has to drop one person to pick up another one."

"Like you dropped me?" I asked.

Birdy looked up from her knitting. Her freckles turned red. "I guess I sorta kinda almost did," she said quietly. "Sorry, Mitzi." We both felt stiff for a minute. "Having one friend at a time is pretty dumb, isn't it?" Birdy said. "I mean like Roxy does."

"It worked OK for you and me," I said.

"Well, we're older now."

That reminded me of my main problem. "Older by the second and running out of time," I said. "So, I've been thinking. If something sad or scary happened, it would probably end my mom's quit, right? I mean, not anything permanently scary. It would just have to upset her long enough to make her light up. All I need is for her to take one puff. One little puff and I'm home free!"

Birdy blinked at me a couple of times, then went back to her knitting (*tap, tap, tap*).

"So, what if we draw a horrible rash on me?" I asked. "Then, after she smokes, we tell her we were just practicing for Halloween!"

"Mitzi!" Birdy scolded without looking up. She was knitting furiously. It was getting on my nerves, so I suggested we go outside to poke around at the church.

"I've got it!" I said. "How about if we fake a kidnapping! I'll hide here at the church. Then, you go to my house and act like you just came over to see me. 'But I thought Mitzi was at YOUR house!' my mom will say, all panicky. Then you say, 'Nope, I haven't seen her all day!' My dad calls 911. The police arrive and flip open their little pads of paper. 'Describe the child, ma'am,' they say. 'What was she wearing when last seen?' At the words *last seen*, my mother will crumble. She'll frantically pat her pockets. No cigarettes. She'll ask the police officers if either of them smokes. One of them does! Mom takes a huge puff and, BINGO! In I walk, casual as a clam. 'What's going on? I was just out for a walk and I heard the siren . . .'"

I looked at Birdy. "So, what do you think?" I asked. She didn't say a word. "Birdy?"

"Mitzi, you're doing it again." Then she held up her hands and wiggled her fingers. A few still had tiny nails growing on them, but the others were gnawed back down to stubs. "Sure is hard to break habits, huh," she sighed.

Birdy could be so annoying.

While I waited for Mom to smoke or not smoke, I secretly quit lying.

When my teacher asked me if I wanted to do the

math problem on the board, I said, "No." When Birdy asked if I liked the wood carving she was doing, I said, "No." When Fern asked if I wanted to come over, I said, "No." And when Mom asked if she looked fat since she'd quit smoking, I said, "Yes." For all the fuss everyone made about honesty, no one seemed to appreciate mine.

Before I knew it, Mom had somehow passed her first smokeless week and was into week number two. She rarely left the house except to teach, but when she was home, she no longer stayed in her room all the time. She even cleaned the fish tank and fixed an occasional dinner.

When it got too tough for her, like when Jake bit a girl on the cheek and broke the skin, Mom went back to bed and watched a video or read something funny. But she still didn't quit her quit. Maybe the tenth time *is* the charm, like Milt said. If that was true, then I was doomed.

On Monday, the fifth-to-the-last day of school, Mike bumped into me in the hall and said, "Hey, Mitzi, look! We're twins!" He poked himself in the chest, pointing to his red T-shirt. I looked down. Yep, mine was red, too. When I looked back up, Mike flashed his gigantic smile at me, and then he turned and walked off. I was too stunned to move. The students parted and surged past me like a river around a rock.

NOW we wear the same shirt? NOW he notices me? NOW he delivers his full, dazzling, ear-to-ear smile? I considered resurrecting my crush, but I just couldn't get my palms to sweat or my knees to go rubbery. Mike Humphrey meant nothing to me.

## 14
## Doomsday and Glug

I felt like a convict awaiting execution, minute by horrible minute. The only one who cared was my prison guard, Birdy. She brought me a crust of stale, moldy bread and some lukewarm water and said, "Boy, I'm sure glad I'm not you!"

There were only two days left. At school I had no idea what we were supposed to be learning, and I kept forgetting which class I had next. Out of school, I couldn't sit still.

Birdy was teaching herself to crochet. I paced her room and watched her digging at the tangled loops of yarn with her crochet hook.

"I am the Royal Court Crocheter making this incredibly gorgeous quilt for the King's baby," Birdy explained. "See? The threads are gold."

I grunted and paced faster.

"No, actually it's that blanket they put on the horse's back," Birdy said. "A perfectly white horse. No, wait, it's a pony, with a silver mane. The Princess has asked me to make this blanket for . . ."

"I don't lie anymore," I reminded her.

"Pretending isn't lying!" Birdy said. "And stop pacing—you're making me nervous."

"Maybe pretending isn't EXACTLY lying, but getting carried away—on a stretcher—has gotten me into a bit of trouble lately, you know. Things get all knotted up and twisted and confused, like your crocheting."

"You don't like my quilt?" Birdy asked in a huff.

I sighed.

"Birdy, you never answered my question. Did you ever pretend with Roxy?" I asked.

"Why?"

"I just want to know," I said.

Birdy rolled her eyes. There was a pause, and then she said, "Kinda, but not the same way. We sort of pretended at the mall. Tried on makeup and clothes like we were actually going to buy them. Stuff like that."

"That's not pretending," I said, "that's practicing!"

"Whatever," Birdy said.

I woke up the next morning and lay in bed listening to the freeway and lawn mower noises, the sweet sounds of my last morning of freedom. Mom came in and hurried me out of bed with her frazzled, late-for-work tone, as if it were just like any other day.

"One more day, then no more Jake!" she sang on her way out the door. All she cared about was herself and HER little problems. No pity for what she was planning to do to ME tomorrow. My mother was cruel, cruel, cruel.

Birdy was waiting outside. We got on the bus and sat with Fern. It was surprisingly brave and loyal of Birdy to sit with me. Fern didn't know any better, but Birdy did. She knew that the next day my mom was going to make me the laughingstock of the school. Birdy was risking contamination just by being seen with me. I wondered if I would have the guts to do the same for her if the roles were ever reversed.

I trudged into school. Fern fell in beside me.

"That girl on the bus is your neighbor, right?" Fern asked.

"Birdy? Yeah," I said.

"She said you never had a dog."

"What? Why were you talking to her about dogs?" I asked nervously.

"And you know what else?" Fern asked.

"Huh?"

"My mom says you couldn't really have a job. You're too young. It would be illegal, unless it was babysitting."

"Oh."

"All you're gonna say is 'oh'?" she sneered. Then, in a really cold voice, she asked, "Well, WAS it babysitting?"

I shrugged, seeing stars in front of my eyes as if I'd been clunked on the head.

"I think something's wrong with you," Fern continued. "I think you should go see a shrink. My mom's a shrink." Fern stopped and looked at me. "Are you crying?"

"No," I lied.

"Why'd you tell me that stuff?" Fern asked. "I don't get it. Wipe your nose."

I wiped my nose on my sleeve.

"Here's my locker," she said and turned away.

I sat very stiff in my seat, feeling dry as dust and brittle as a stick. I knew that if I moved too quickly, or something bumped me, I'd snap. It has begun, I thought. This is what the rest of my life will be like. Fern was just the first to scorn me, and she didn't even know about the Stripitis lie yet.

When my eyes and brain had cleared a little, I noticed Vanessa sitting a few seats away. She looked droopy. That's when it dawned on me that her dad really did have cancer and that she'd gone through all that hospital stuff *for real*. Wow. I wondered if Vanessa's class had made cards for her dad when he got sick. We'd gone to different elementary schools then, so I didn't know.

On the way to P.E., I caught up with Vanessa and asked if her dad was OK.

"My dad?"

"Well, you look kind of sad," I said.

"My dad's fine," she said.

"Oh." I started to walk away.

"It's something else," she called after me, and I turned around. "It's Michael," she whispered in my ear. "He likes someone else now."

"Michael? You mean Mike Humphrey?" I asked. "Who's the girl?"

Vanessa shrugged. "I don't know, but he asked her to be his girlfriend and she's thinking about it."

"Thinking about it?" I asked, and I knew that Roxy Gold-crud had struck again!

"But even if she decides not to be his girlfriend,

Michael doesn't like *me* anymore." Vanessa looked miserable.

"It was his wide smile that got you, wasn't it?" I asked. "The way his mouth opens so far?"

"How did you know?"

I said, "You and I have a lot in common."

See how life is? I thought. Now that I kind of liked Vanessa, she'd find out about the lie and hate me for sure.


Fern sat way across the bus from me on the ride home. I stared out the window. At my door, Birdy said, "Good luck." But I could tell she thought I needed much more than luck. My time was up.

I trudged through the house and stood outside my parents' bedroom door. I could hear the Roadrunner's *meep, meep* coming from their TV. My cold, heartless parents were in there laughing their heads off—without a thought for how they were about to destroy my life. I wanted to run and hide, disappear in a cloud of cartoon dust, just like the Roadrunner.

Could it really have been only twenty-five days since Mom and I shook hands on this awful deal? It felt like I'd spent YEARS dreading this moment. I was almost relieved that the suspense was finally over. I was sure that another minute of this agony would reduce me to a drooling, babbling heap of twitches. So I squared my shoulders, took a deep breath, and knocked on the door.

They both SMILED at me when I walked in, as if everything was just peachy! For a split second I thought maybe they'd forgotten what day it was. Maybe I could tiptoe through the next twenty-four hours until school was out. Pretend I'd miscounted the days of Mom's quit. By the time they remembered, it would be summer vacation—and too late!

Instead, I whispered, "You win."

Mom rubbed her hands together and cackled wicked-witch style.

"Tomorrow's the last day of school," I said.

"I know," she said, patting the bed next to her for me to sit down. I was too nervous to sit.

"So, tomorrow . . . class confession?" I asked.

"You've been pardoned," Dad said. "Your merciful parents have shown pity on you."

"Huh?" That was me.

"Well," Dad continued, "do you regret that lie, THOSE lies, more than anything in the world?"

"Yes . . ."

"And you've quit lying forever and ever?" asked my mother.

I was about to say yes, but instead, I said, "I'm trying."

"Well, that's a start," she smiled. "We release you."

"What?"

"My quit is going great," Mom said. "And it's mostly your doing, Mitzi. You shamed me into it. And besides, how could I possibly stand in front of a room full of strange kids and tell them I'm a lousy mother and my daughter is a liar—without a cigarette? That would take a half a pack, at least!"

I looked at her. She was smiling.

"You mean we're NOT doing it? For real?"

"Well, unless you absolutely insist!" Mom said. "But I think we could skip it."

My dad nodded and said, "We suspect you've punished yourself pretty thoroughly. You've had a hunted-rabbit look on your face for weeks now."

Then my parents looked at each other and giggled. Huh? They were *laughing* at me?

Wait a minute—Les was RIGHT! They'd been bluffing all along! They'd enjoyed watching me squirm. I couldn't believe they'd made me sweat it out all those weeks for nothing.

I was about to complain, but then I remembered how much worse off I'd be at that moment if it *hadn't* all been for nothing! My anger fizzed away, like little bubbles rising in a can of Mountain Dew. *Pop!* Gone.

"We won't cover for you, you know," Dad said.

"If anyone asks us ANYTHING about Mom's health, we absolutely won't lie. Got it?"

"Yes!"

"And if we hear that you've let this lie go an inch further, you're in deep trouble," Mom added.

"Thank you, thank you, thank you!" That was me, thrilled to bits. I jumped on the bed and gave them each an enormous hug. Then my whole body went from stiff with fear to rubbery with relief. I felt like a bathtub with the plug pulled—all the dirty water going around and around, down the drain with a *glug!*

My brain chanted, "It's over, it's over!" And I knew my tongue would knot and cramp, my teeth would crumble, and my lips would melt like candles before another lie like that would ever come out of me again.

I called Birdy as soon as I could and told her the good news. She squawked, "What? They were just KIDDING?"

I laughed. "Yup."

"No way, Mitzi!" she squealed. "You're lying."

"Not this time," I replied, and I'd never been so glad to be telling the truth.

# Amy Goldman Koss

*Then*

*Now*

Amy Goldman Koss really does have a best friend named Birdy. As girls, they loved to play pretend and meet in front of the church between their houses. Amy, like her character Mitzi, was known sometimes to stretch the truth, but her active imagination later helped her write many well-known books, including *The Ashwater Experiment* and *How I Saved Hanukkah.* Her greatest accomplishment, however, was kicking her own smoking habit while writing *Smoke Screen.* She's still smoke-free today and living in Glendale, California, with her husband and two children.